Voices, Visions and Dreams: An Anthology

Voices, Visions and Dreams: An Anthology

Compiled by

Sharon Freeman Laborde

Cahaba Press

Eureka Springs, Arkansas

USA

Cahaba Press
483 CR 231
Eureka Springs, AR 72631
www.cahabapublishing.com

Cover photograph by Mariellen Griffith

ISBN: 9798776696527

Dedication

This selection of essays, stories and poetry is dedicated to St. Jude Children's Research Hospital, Memphis, Tennessee, whose ground breaking work in saving the lives of so many will never be forgotten. All proceeds from the sale of this book will benefit the hospital.

Table of Contents

My Last Adventure

By

Fred Norrell

We left Scotland bound for the American colonies when I was too young to comprehend it all. Some bits of Scotland remain in my memory, but I particularly recall that warm summer eve in 1745, when Da came home from his shop early, worried by news that Bonnie Prince Charlie had come ashore in our Northwest and raised an army to unseat King George II. With uncomfortable silence, Maw took in the news, her eyes down, her lips drawn firm. I had questions, but was afraid to speak. In the days that followed, Da told us of the army's progress to the South. I could feel tension on the rise in our neighborhood, but I didn't understand much of it. Glasgow was a fair place to live, a bonnie spot in Scotland, I was told. So why would anyone attack Glasgow? And what would occur during an attack? How would our lives change? Later, I understood more; in our home of Glasgow, factory folk, tradespeople and shopkeepers were Whigs, in support of the British King. We were Scots but also British, a political arrangement that had brought to us more trade and more to our tables. In Glasgow, life was always moving. Ships went out to sea with cargo: ploughs, hand tools, stoves, cookware and all sorts of manufactured wares. On carts, these were transported through the streets to ships at the docks, recurrently filling the city with traffic. Likewise, ships came in bearing tobacco, corn, cotton and lumber. Carts conveyed it to the city's warehouses, so we frequently found our streets in a lively state. This was a new Scotland, and did not sit well with Bonnie Prince Charlie, who held loyal to a past of independent Highland warriors … giants of an age gone by.

Then it came like thunder. Bonnie Prince Charlie marched on Edinburgh with an army of ferocious, sword-wielding clansmen, demanding surrender. Almost at once the city's defenses seemed to evaporate, and the invaders occupied Edinburgh in September. Not to be denied, the British assembled an army at Prestonpans, just east of the capital, only to scatter in terror as Charlie's army attacked, screaming and waving swords and battleaxes. Townspeople said Glasgow was next. I could see fear in Maw's eyes and those of our neighbors. Da didn't speak much; he appeared deep in thought. And now I felt fear of Bonnie Prince Charlie. Somehow I knew Da could not stop him. I imagined a giant with sword in one hand, axe in the other, smiting our neighbors left and right. My fear was greatest when Da and Maw started packing our household belongings. Da brought home a packing crate, and we wrapped items in clothing and stuffed them in. Da packed his smaller cooper's tools, and Maw packed her small cooking ware and some sewing things. I packed my knife and slingshot. We left behind all kinds of things: pots and pans, brooms, dust feathers, older clothes and some things I had not noticed before. Lastly, Maw put some food in small sacks.

It was a misty chill October day when we left the house, neighbors bidding us farewell and taking the remains of our wares. A man was there to collect the house key and paid Da some money. It was sure strange; I didn't know where we would go, and I was wide awake, having wild imaginings, and they wouldn't stop. A cart carried us to the docks where we stood in wait a goodly time. Da was talking with people on a ship and Maw kept me close by. I asked if we were getting on a ship; she smiled and put her arm around me. At last, our crate was taken onto the ship floating just before us. Da returned and said we would be travelling on that vessel. As Da later told me, he had days before made arrangements to depart Scotland, and so we did on that day in October, boarding a ship bound for the American colonies.

We were instructed to collect our belongings and follow. Across the dock we passed small groupings of people, all of them excited and speaking rather loudly, nervously it seemed. Crossing a small bridge connected to the ship, I noticed it rose and fell gently with the water. On the ship, I felt it move in the same way. My first time on a ship ... it was a bit scary, but I discovered I liked it! We were escorted below deck, dimly lit with a few lanterns, and shown our assigned space. A rope was tied around our quarters and hammocks were hung—one for each of us. When not used for sleeping the hammocks would come down, leaving just enough space to sit, eat, and other things. One of the ship's important laws was to put all waste in our assigned bucket, dispose of it quickly overboard, and never pish anywhere else.

Our space was dreadfully cramped and seemed to shrink as more and more people came down from the deck. Most looked like folk from our city, with neat leather shoes and clean clothes. Ladies wore bonnets, some with a flower. Children were wide-eyed and wore looks of uncertainty. I own they, like me, were aboard ship for the first time. We were packed close together and the talking was loud and the air smelled hot and musty. Our family was one among many, and there was no room below deck to do anything. After quite some time waiting in this steaming noisy Hell, I felt the ship move in a different way—we had left the dock. The ship leaned over gently, and I could see people leaning the opposite way. Then it righted, and we did too. Then another lean and another. All this was gentle for a good part of the day; then the ship hit open water and the movements became more sudden and forceful. Some souls cried out. These harsh motions stayed with us on our crossing of the Atlantic, and many people were sick, frequently using their buckets.

Da was looking at me; our eyes met. He began, "We are leaving behind our Scotland, where I have lived for all my life, and so my parents and grandparents, and on back in days past. I don't favor leaving, but it has become a danger for us." I nodded. "You have heard about Bonnie Prince Charlie, I know." Another nod. "I think a good place to live will be the American colonies. You will find friends there, Scottish lads I'll wager. And I've been told there are good schools in those colonies." With some

4

effort I managed a smile. "This voyage takes us across the Atlantic Ocean." Here, Maw looked up, her face showing some anxiety. "And I expect it will be seven or eight weeks before we see land again. We must all," and here he looked at Maw and back to me, "keep up our mettle and hope for the best." Slowly, Maw's head dropped and turned away, and Da put his hand on her shoulder. He turned my way; we nodded in understanding.

I could not be kept below deck. On deck I had to be watchful and stay clear from the sailors, as they handled ropes and sails, rushing here and there. The sails were interesting, or rather the use of them. Most of the time wind came from the Northeast, and the sails filled out to the left. When the wind abated the sails would begin to relax and hang loose. Crew would be on the watch, and sometimes move the sails to the other side of the ship; ropes would be untied, moved around and tied in new positions. The crew watched attentively, alert for signs of changing winds. The sails might hang relaxed for a few moments before billowing out with fresh breeze. All this kept the sailors busy.

But the sea—the sea was a marvel to behold. At times I held my breath. The water was alternately deep blue, then green, then gray, and usually tipped with white foam. I watched the waves for hours. The sky was other than the one that looked down upon Glasgow, clouds moving so fast that if you looked away for a moment or two the scene had changed completely. Storms came up suddenly, and at those times I retreated below deck. Calm days found me watching crewmembers fishing. They would

5

simply throw out baited lines that dragged behind ship. Then the line would grow taut and move about. I was surprised to see the crewmen pull the lines in by hand, but they managed. I saw some of the strangest fish ever; and some were thrown back into the beautiful waters, but most were carried to the galley. Sometimes a fish was so big the line had to be cut loose.

I stayed on deck almost every day until the day I got sick. Many were affected by the ship's movements, but a different malady had now made itself known. I had a fever, as did Maw. Still, she gave me food and water and freshened my clothes. If Da had fever he was hiding it. Some unfortunates died and had to be dropped into the sea, wrapped in cloth. I remember little after that ... except for the bucket. When I had the strength, my job was to carry it up to deck and empty it over the rail into the sea. At times I hardly had the energy to do so, and I had to be careful to avoid dropping it. The crossing became a long, miserable affair. We endured.

After a lifetime, we arrived at Perth Amboy, Colony of New Jersey in early December. At first, stepping on solid ground was disorienting and caused new feelings of illness. Crowds packed the docks and streets, all in a rush with calling out and yelling. I felt lost and could not imagine how we would find our way to wherever we were going. We were still a bit sick and weak. We were approached by a few people; Scots, I could hear by their accents. They were a welcoming group, helping new arrivals. They got for us lodgings and a meal for the night, and Maw cried. She saw I was watching and put her arms around me. "You are my brave one and it lifts my heart to see it. I have tears, Love, tears of joy. We have survived our passage across a terrible ocean, and now we are met with kind people and given a place to rest. And rest we should. Please stay close." I was overcome with fatigue, but when our new friends returned with tea, biscuits, bacon and apples, we ate. Then came a deep sleep. I could hear footsteps now and again, but quickly descended again into sleep. I was walking alone on the ship's deck, a brilliant emerald ocean lay before me, rising and falling in great, smooth mountains of water. A fresh breeze caressed my face and billowed the sails, carrying smells of the sea. I breathed deeply. No land in sight, only a vast sweep of blue-green in motion. After a few minutes of this splendor, my steps took me to the ship's bow where I turned to my left, to be greeted by quite another sight; low in the sky, in fact hugging the water, lurked a huge, nasty black cloud. It boiled and squirmed, arms reaching then retracting, as if to grab the unwary sailor. A cold gale suddenly assaulted my whole being. Emerald faded into dark grey, and the waves transformed into sharp, violent monsters, ripping at the ship's side. The vessel rocked violently from side to side, tossing me over the rail into the icy black … I awoke with a start.

We remained in our room a few days more, gradually recovering from the voyage. Then a move from the town center to a house, or part of a house shared with a family of Scots. We had our rooms and they theirs. Maw had to buy cooking wares and food. She would call on me to help carry her purchases, so I learned the streets near our house. There were warehouses filled with tobacco, the smell filling the streets. There were sawmills and ship building shops, their loud work assaulting the ears. Many people in town were Scots, but English soldiers marched through the streets every day, crowds parting to let them pass. Da found work at a cooper's shop, and I was sent to a school with mostly English instructors. Over the next two years, as Maw said, I spoke more and more like an Englishman. At the house we shared, I worked in the garden though winter had set in and the main task consisted of soil preparation for spring planting. I learned how to ready a garden, first to clear it so insects would not stay, then to amend the soil with vegetable matter and manure. I learned how to chop and split firewood better, and my job was to supply our stove. Soon I was tasked with keeping the stove alight, which meant getting out of bed at night to add fresh wood to the fire. My jobs kept me tethered to earth; otherwise I would have been lost.

Da was a good cooper and progressed at the shop, becoming one of the master coopers. He promised to teach me when I was older. He and Maw must have been saving money, because after a little more than two years we were ready to move. Only Maw did not want to get on a ship. I remember she cried, but finally agreed to sail down to Norfolk, Virginia. We packed up again, but kept more things this time, and our belongings filled a few crates. A wagon carried our crates to the docks and we walked along side; it was a good long walk. There was no waiting at the dock; we went onto the ship, and found a reasonable space for our living needs. We were accompanied by just a few other passengers, but quite a few crates and barrels. I was surprised the ship cast off as soon as it did. We hit rough waters soon thereafter, and the dreaded rocking and pounding of the ship brought back memories of our Atlantic crossing. I hated it. Fortunately, the trip was only a couple of days. We stepped off the ship onto the docks of Norfolk, what was to be our new home.

Again, we were greeted by a welcoming committee, and they directed us to lodgings for the night. Next day, as I stepped out onto the street I encountered clear, fresh smelling air. I knew we had found a good place to call home. The streets were not so crowded as with Perth Amboy, and the pace of traffic more relaxed. We had to find new lodgings, so we walked about the town. At first we settled on a room close in, affording me a chance to explore the town. But we moved again in a few weeks' time. We now live in a community a half mile from the town's edge. Maw got her garden, and I got my old jobs of gardening, firewood and stove.

Da had brought his cooper's tools and set up his own shop at the mouth of Chesapeake Bay. Da had me in school until I was fifteen, and then began my cooper's apprenticeship. We manufactured wooden barrels and kegs, but other items were natural sides: like buckets, baskets, crates, tool handles and firewood. We had two wood acquisition teams, lumber being dear, and I was assigned to one. Robert and I went out into the forests to acquire white oak and pine. We drove a mule named Daisy, with her chain for dragging the tree trunks behind.

9

The best barrels – for food and drink – are made of white oak, which has a remarkably straight grain in the trunk. Search and identification was not difficult, because the oak leaves are as large as a hand and show a smooth, wavy profile around the lobes and sinuses. We would search for good straight trees, Robert making notes on his map. When we found a tree best for harvest, Robert would inspect the surroundings, decide on the direction of felling, and set up the saw. He was in his twenties, bigger and stronger than me, so he could put a good pull on the whipsaw. I had to learn to pace myself, otherwise I would not last the day. First, we cut a V-shape into the trunk, about waist high, knock out the loose piece, remove the saw to the other side and cut horizontally until our tree came down.

Rarely did we fell a tree without having to rest. Lunch was in the forest. By late afternoon we would have felled a tree, cut at least one log about thirteen feet long, rolled it onto the dragging chain and secured it. We watered Daisy and washed ourselves and took a rest before setting off for the shop. On the way back, staying on trails, the most important things were to rest Daisy, avoid dips in the ground, watch one's feet, and to keep the log tightly secured. When the log got stuck, we would have to roll it side to side while trying to keep Daisy pulling. Sometimes we would have to unhitch Daisy, lead her to the log's other end, and back away from the dip. It was all hard work. At the shop, Robert and Da would inspect the log, commenting on its merits or weak points, then roll it to the drying yard, where I affixed a date tag.

On the next day we would return to our tree and collect more logs. Pine was a bit easier to collect because there were more pine trees, and pine is not as heavy as oak. Some barrels, like for tobacco, are made from pine; also, pine is useful for crates and baskets. This was my life for the next several years. I learned a lot, like making tool handles, crates, baskets and buckets—buckets that would hold water. Most importantly, I had learned how to make barrels. Da, being a patient teacher, showed me one trick after another in the art of making a good barrel. Logs were split into staves—small boards as long as the height of a barrel. Staves were placed on a cooper's plane—a flat, smooth wood surface with an angled blade sticking through. The angle is such that when the staves are run across, they will fit together to form a tight seam when assembled into a barrel. The ends of the staves had to be cut a little deeper than at the middle, one of the skills that made a good cooper.

Da was smart. Not only was he a master cooper and good businessman, he understood politics and people. Farmers needed barrels to pack tobacco or corn to be shipped to Great Britain. They bargained with Da to little effect. He knew about all the trade laws and related taxes, and knew how to adjust our production: barrels or kegs, oak or pine. I don't know how he did it, but we rarely had unsold or unclaimed wares in the shop. Da knew a lot of neighbors, most of them English, and some evenings they would gather on our street, exchanging news and complaints. Gripes were plenty, due to a continual introduction of new laws and taxes imposed by the Brits.

We were losing our loyalty to the British Parliament and Crown. When tempers flared, Da would step in and find the words to ease things. I think the neighbors looked up to him. I did. Maw was a natural at making friends, and some of them had daughters. They helped one another with everyday chores, and often shared company. She was still sickly, and never had any more children, and I think that weighed upon her. But we were settled and happy in our new life.

In August 1764, I met Captain Patrick at Southey's Tavern. I had ambled in one evening after a hot day at the shop. Southey's was one of the more peaceful places to get an ale, and I came there with greater and greater frequency. Other taverns were dark, but I liked looking out Southey's windows as I sat and enjoyed my ale. I saw the town folk pass by in unguarded moments, and enjoyed seeing their faces. The Captain was tall, half a head over me, well proportioned, with reddish hair on head and chin. His eyes revealed a playful sense of humor, and his lips appeared ready to speak at any moment. This held my attention, even in intervals of silence. He spoke with an easy, natural authority. I felt comfortable in his company, and we readily exchanged observations and opinions.

Over a tankard of ale he remarked, "I've seen ye about. Work at the cooper's do ye?" I nodded. "I've handled yer barrels on occasion." I explained that Da was the chief cooper.

"Yer Da, eh? Mine, if he lives, should find him in Scotland still." We talked about Scotland; he was from the North and East of Glasgow, out in the countryside, had worked a potato farm. I asked what brought him to the colonies.

"Dunno, really. Years back, I was young, poor harvests ... and what brings you?"

I recited a short version of my life story, while the Captain listened carefully, nodding now and again. He interjected "You know any young women?" There were few around and free, and of course he knew that; we laughed.

"I knew a lass lived up the bay. She was a Scot to beat all! Smoked a pipe and drank rum as good as myself, and in argument gave no quarter. Lifted her skirts alright, and we saw much alike. Last I saw her, her Da came for myself with a blade. I stuck a leg in me trousers, but had to then run, shoes in one hand, trousers in the other. Villagers got a good look at me backside, I'll wager."

I laughed so that ale found its way into my nose. Choking and gasping, I held up my hand to stop the hilarity. Rising, the Captain clapped my back, yet we laughed the more. He ordered two ales, and shoved mine over. We drank still another and talked into the late evening.

"Yes, I'm in the trades" he said. "My wee boat has borne many a barrel of molasses to these shores and up river. The James is not always kind to these big ships. Sometimes trades take me up the bay."

"Is it only molasses you trade?" I ventured. Here, he paused, looking closely into my eyes. I blurted "Sorry ... I should not have ..."

He relaxed, "It's a fair query; I have been changing

13

cargo as of late."

He told me about the Sugar Act. In April 1764 the British Parliament passed a law that forbade the importation of "foreign" rum into the colonies. British rum was dear and French rum from the Caribbean was cheap. So, his current cargo was, of course, French rum. We cursed the Brits on this and a number of other matters.

"So, are ye game?" he surprised me with the invitation.

I asked, "What would come to me?"

"I run a wee boat, and the two of us can handle her in fair weather. I get a share, the boat, she gets a share, and you get a share of the three. You see, the cargo is ready; and me mate has taken the fever, and I fear he is done."

I explained my work at the shop and that I was free only at nights. Why was I explaining? I don't know why I was interested; I was making money at the shop, living on the cheap, and saving on the side. Looking back, I think it was nothing more than my appetite for adventure. Unmarried, with no serious prospects, I agreed to be a partner in a 'run.' We discussed details.

On the night of the run I came to the pier on Little Creek, finding Captain Patrick where he had said. He was rather business-like, working in the boat, and spoke little other than to acknowledge my arrival. His boat resembled others I had seen: about twenty feet long, wide at the beam, with a rather short mast. On both sides were pegs to support the oars. We set to work organizing the lines, sail and oars. I could feel excitement growing in anticipation of this adventure and was ready to go.

My thoughts were interrupted when two fellows rushed

up to the pier, urgently declaring we had to depart at once. Captain Patrick apparently knew them and gave the order to get aboard and cast off. He and I pushed the boat out into the creek and took up the oars. The two passengers huddled down, hiding their faces, and this caused me some concern. A bit of rowing brought us to the open misty waters of Chesapeake Bay. I could see lanterns by the far shoreline, their lights undulating on the water's smooth surface. The water was quite calm, smelling of salt water and fish. We rowed for another distance and the water became rougher, whereupon the Captain ordered me to raise sail, while he took the tiller. The wind was from the Northeast, so we made for the Southeast. We then tacked back North, then back and forth, making our way generally to the East. After what seemed like about an hour the Captain lit a lantern and we continued our tacking. Through the fog a light appeared and we sailed toward an uncertain destination, our two passengers increasingly watchful. The outlines of a ship gradually manifested in our view. We approached.

Rugged looking men peered over the ship's rail, musket barrels staring at us, which set my heart to pounding. Captain Patrick called out his name, was answered by way of a riddle, and replied, whereupon we were ordered to come alongside the ship. Another verbal exchange was followed by the lowering of a wide rope ladder, which Captain Patrick climbed. I could see he had done this before, as he nimbly leaped over the rail. A moment later some loud arguing was overheard, and finally the two passengers were ordered to come aboard. They were questioned heatedly, and as best I could hear, required to pay ... probably passenger fee. After tempers eased, I could hear Captain Patrick bargaining for the purchase of rum and directly a small rope ladder appeared with a keg in its fold. As the ladder was played out, the keg descended into our boat. Leaning over the ships rail, Captain Patrick directed me as to its handling. Five more kegs followed, then the Captain. We stored our cargo in the prow of his boat, cut loose from the ship, raised sail, and began our journey back to shore, no lantern.

After only 30 minutes or so we heard another boat; we lowered sail and remained as quiet as we could manage. The Captain's eyes revealed his intensity. Again, my heart was pounding. The British customs boat, lanterns aplenty, passed behind us, which was fortunate because the wind apparently prevented the British soldiers from hearing the waves lapping upon the side of our boat. As they disappeared into the fog we raised sail and continued our journey. Some faint lights somehow guided the Captain to our destination. We dropped sail and manned the oars, pulling our way back to the pier.

At once British soldiers rushed upon us, shouting, muskets at the ready. As I stepped onto the pier, I received one musket butt to the ribs, then one to the jaw. Dazed, I was dragged a short distance, made to stand, then stumbled some distance, finally arriving at a jail of sorts. Behind bars I found myself in the company of a few rough looking fellows who, thankfully, ignored my arrival. An hour later Captain Patrick joined us, and I was glad of his company. Unlike me, he had been questioned by the Brits. A few minutes later we were informed that we were accused of aiding two men who had attempted to shoot Lt. Governor Fauquier. A third assailant had been wounded and captured. The two we had transported to the ship were wanted for the crime. This was more than I had in the bargain, and I felt anger and fear at the same moment. The next morning Da came to see me at the jail, and questioned me about my ill-fated adventure. I could sense he was a bit angry with me, but I received no lecture.

Captain Patrick and I were taken to a hearing room the next day, where he denied knowing the passengers or anything about them. He plead guilty to smuggling rum and was fined but represented that six kegs amounted to a minor transgression. I made the same plea, and Da testified that I had not done such a thing before. We were sentenced to work gangs, the Captain to two months, me one. For the first time I saw a look of defeat in Da's eyes, and my heart sank. What had I done?

During that time I worked with a crew dredging the North bank of the James River. Large buckets were used to scoop out the mud. I volunteered that I knew how to make buckets, and was assigned bucket repair. My work was not hard and the summer heat was beginning to lift; mornings brought fresh breezes. The work gang consisted of a variety of characters, most of which were downcast and looked dangerous. I quickly learned not to ask for anything, lest I anger the soldiers or the prisoners. Nights brought a worry. None of us had anything to steal, other than shoes, but in the dark of our meager quarters I could

17

hear stirrings. The older gang members stayed to themselves, and avoided confrontation. One of the younger fellows was full of himself and pushed others around. I avoided him. His tenure was terminated by a shovel to the back of the head. There was blood a-plenty; his attacker was easily identified, beaten and dragged off. The injured was loaded on a wagon and, thankfully, not seen again. Now, gang members were quiet for the most part, but from time to time they exploded with curses and flying fists. It was rather frightening because some of them were clearly good at fighting.

I had never wanted to fight and had avoided it without too much effort, until one day a section of bucket I was repairing fell on the foot of a brash young fellow who immediately punched me on the side of the head. I stumbled to the side and fell and was overcome with dizziness. My attacker began kicking me in the side, so I had to move. I rolled into the river, away from the bank. I scooped up a handful of mud, and as my attacker closed upon me, threw it into his eyes. The soldiers were upon us in a flash, and were none too gentle. Fortunately one of them had witnessed the whole affair and defended my actions.

He took my arm, a slim fellow with a kind face, and advised, "Be warned, some of my mates are a bit rough. I see your head took a blow; a handful of cool mud should not hurt it. I observe you are getting on well with the buckets. Take yourself a rest while we chat, but first the mud."

I knew about the mud, but was not thinking clearly. He

was from east London, the low side, but spoke with what I understood to be good English, well almost. A junior officer in charge of the river detail, he was on his first tour outside of Britain. I told him of my adventure with rum-running and it was received with quite a few laughs. He was a fine fellow; I wish I had gotten his name. I returned to my work. I think this episode ended as well as could be expected, but I had painful bruises on head and ribs. After the first few slow days the month passed faster than I had reason to hope, and upon release I determined to avoid trouble of any nature.

Back to life as a free man. My parents welcomed me back, especially Maw.

Da sat me down and began, "You have started." I had no thought as to what that meant. "When a person starts with an act of crime or hurt, he can easily try it again, and with each act it all comes with ease, it becomes one's way in life. And now you have started, and you must decide if you will allow it to happen again, or if you will guard against it." I started to speak, but he held up his hand. "Out in the water, out in that boat, you could have been shot, you could have died. Think on that."

Hearing this, my thoughts froze; I had nothing to say. Da stood and put his hand on my shoulder. I looked up into his caring eyes, stood and hugged him. Maw had listened to all this, and when I turned, she pleaded "Please take care of yourself, my only son."

The next day, Da put me to work at the shop and largely ignored me. I fell into the rhythm of work, gladly breathing the cool air of early fall. After some weeks we had a new customer: a distiller, who needed barrels for molasses and kegs for rum. That meant more oak, and I was given plenty of work. The seasons went by and we stayed busy. These days Da walks around the shop, checking the quality of work and keeping the books. Robert had become a master cooper, and I was next in line. Life was good, lots of business and friends at the shop. I rose early, but not so as to find Maw in her sleep. She had warmed a thick slice of bread with butter and honey, tea as well. As I ate her gaze rested upon me. A kiss on the cheek and a word or two, and I was off to open the shop. We tidy before closing, but there was always more to be done. Among other tasks, I tended to Daisy and Rose, her stable mate; then I fire up the chimney place, set the big kettle to warm, and gather kindling and fuel for the barrel firing station. Da, Robert and our apprentices, all good fellows, arrive one by one. Da rarely made assignments; we knew what to do.

The years passed, during which I met some interesting lassies. My life was getting quite exciting, but bigger issues were afoot. Tensions had grown and then some. We had come to reject the authority of British law. After the Sugar Act came the Stamp Act, and Quartering Act, which required colonists to provide room and board for British soldiers. Colonists declared there should be no taxes levied in the absence of our voice being heard. As tensions grew, we heard about the Boston Tea Party; the Brits responded by closing Boston harbor and fortifying the city.

Fall 1774 – The First Continental Congress assembled

in Philadelphia to express our grievances and adopt plans to cope with the British. Then war: the following April the Brits defeated our minutemen in Lexington, colony of Massachusetts. In Concord, not far distant, the battle's outcome was not as clear, but as the Brits removed themselves toward Boston, they were ambushed from all sides and sustained heavy losses. The Battle of Bunker Hill saw clear results; the Brits were driven back to Boston. In Virginia the Brits smashed Norfolk's printing press, the main voice speaking of British malfeasance. There was a large protest, or it might be considered a revolt, and the British soldiers were moved out of town. A few days later they reappeared in great numbers, threatening and bullying whoever was met. Some of our neighbors were beaten rather badly. Our minutemen formed and patrolled the streets. Danger hung in the air. War exploded in Virginia in November, with the capture of eighteen colonists, and the deaths of seven. I knew some of these lads, and my heart sank.

Friends and neighbors urged me to join the fighting, so the next militia meeting found me in attendance. I was among the older ones, but not experienced in shooting. I thusly refused an offer to lead a group of the militiamen. I volunteered to the repair of wagons and other equipment and was assigned command of those functions. I felt well prepared and accepted with confidence. I felt a rush of pride in purpose; then I thought of Maw and Da.

Returning home, Da saw it in my eyes, took my arm, and we sat. He began, "I had hoped, as we all did, that we could find a good life here. But the British are set to rule our lives and tax every bob from our pockets. Without we take a stand, we will not have a life worthy of free men. I see no satisfactory path before us; war is upon us. I fear for our lives and this whether you join the militia or no."

His eyes were at once thoughtful and saddened. I put my hand on his ageing arm, an arm that had guided me for all my days. I was thankful we had reached this understanding. My courage was renewed, and this must have been visible, for Da's eyes brightened with pride. Our handshake was warm and seemed to fix our resolve.

Maw, dear woman, was of few words. Her eyes, her face told of her heart's desires. Such were the eyes upon me now that my feelings rushed upon me with sudden unexpected power.

"My only son, always my brave one, you have made our family whole. My illness after your birth meant no children would follow. But you have completed our family in so many ways. I know you are a man, a good man, and my heart goes with you. May you keep safe as best you can."

Speechless, I nodded and brought her into my arms. My heart bursting, I took a deep breath; the smell of her greying hair was our farewell.

Now on to the militia camp. And I thought rum running was my last adventure!

Fred Norrell is a retired economist, living with his wife, Renée, in Virginia. A native of Alabama, he is the author of *A Boy's Adventures on Lake Martin*. His current interests are music, Tai Chi, and being a grandfather.

Looking Good All the Way to the End:

A Memoir

By

Zeek Taylor

Where I come from in the Upper Arkansas Delta, funerals are considered an important part of "living." In that region and especially among the older generation, there are honored traditions concerning funerals with little variation. The traditions include visitation with the family at the funeral home, usually with an open casket so the body can be viewed one last time. The funeral service is then held the following day in either the funeral home or a church. Following the service there is a slow moving procession of mourners in cars with headlights beaming on the way to the cemetery for a graveside service. While all this is going on, there is much socializing, and the bereaved family is gifted with enough home cooked food to feed an army.

When I was a kid, there was a woman who lived in my small town who enjoyed attending funerals. If there was not a funeral to attend of someone that she knew, she would go to services for strangers. She would listen to the obits on the radio every morning, and she often would attend any funeral that was in driving distance of her

23

home. She averaged one or two funerals a week.

Women in my mother's beauty shop would discuss funerals with particular attention paid to how good the body looked. The appearance of the body seemed important to them. They discussed whether the embalmed person looked "natural" and what the deceased was wearing. "Did they have on their jewelry and how did their hair look?"

My mother worked as a hairdresser for more than 60 years. During that time many of her customers passed away and at the request of the family of the deceased, she would go to the funeral home to do the hair of the departed so they would look good for the viewing. Although I don't know how she did it, my mother wanted her customers who had passed to look natural and to look good. It was always upsetting to my mother to do that service for the family, but she considered it a part of her job. Perhaps to lighten the situation a little, she would jokingly say, "At least I don't have to worry about how the back of their hair looks."

My mother knew exactly how she wanted her funeral, and she planned every detail years before it took place. She wrote down in a notebook the songs she wanted to be played during the service and the names of pallbearers, along with an alternate list in case one or more of the preferred had preceded her in death. She wrote down the color of the spray of flowers that she wanted to be on top of the casket. She prepaid for everything, including the casket that she had selected herself. The only thing she did not pick out was what she would be wearing. She said to the family, "I might buy something prettier to wear between now and then, and y'all can choose."

The call came early one January morning in 2002. My mother at the age of 88 had died while she was getting dressed for work. I immediately packed and rushed across state. I needed to be home. The family gathered the next morning at the funeral home to make arrangements with not much to do since my mother had taken care of everything. We did take a recently purchased outfit for her to wear. It was the dress I had given her a couple of weeks earlier at Christmas.

While making the arrangements, the undertaker asked, "And who do you want to do her hair?" I found myself saying, "I will do it." I had been styling her hair for years, and I couldn't bear for anyone else to do it. I knew that my mother would want it to be perfect. It was one of the hardest things I've ever done, but it was very important for me to do it. I knew that it was the last thing that I could do for my mother.

She looked good.

Zeek Taylor is a recipient of the Arkansas Governor's Art Award for Lifetime Achievement, and his paintings have hung in the Arkansas Governor's Mansion. He is also a storyteller and writer who has performed twice on the National Public Radio show *Tales From the South.* Taylor's third book, *Out of the Delta II* was published in early 2021.

https://www.zeektaylor.com

The Square Root of Family

By

Charles L. Templeton

In the spring of 1956, my mother received a phone call from my grandmother. We lived in California, where my dad was stationed at Edwards Air Force Base in the Mojave Desert. I was ten years old, my little brother was five, and my older sister was fifteen going on thirty. My sister was usually off with her friends listening to Elvis Presley, who was all the rage among teenage girls. So, my little brother and I spent hours exploring the desert that surrounded the base with a neighbor's kid, Gene Fiaconni. Gene was an expert at finding tortoises and various snakes, and he knew which ones to avoid.

My mom and my grandmother usually communicated with letters since my grandmother was living back in Texas, long-distance phone calls in our family were rare because of the expense. We usually only talked with our grandparents on holidays and special occasions. My little brother, Jimmy, and I were watching the *Cisco Kid* when the phone rang. Of course, when we heard that Mom was talking to Grandmom, we were so excited we started jumping up and down. My little brother was laughing and yelling, "Oh, Cisco!' and I was laughing and yelling, "Oh, Pancho!" Our mom was unsuccessfully trying to shush us.

It was total mayhem in our tiny kitchen. She finally resorted to those magic words kids have been responding to for years, "Wait until your dad gets home."

Our mom's mother was our favorite relative and always spoiled us when we were with her. Of course, it was easy to spoil a child back then. You just said, "Why don't you kids go on outside and play. You can do your chores later." So, as you might imagine, we loved staying at Grandmother's house. It was a different time, and we always finished our chores.

One of my grandmother's closest friends from church had died suddenly, and my grandmother was distraught. This woman who had passed away had taken care of my mom, on occasion, when she was growing up. My grandmother and her friend, Louise, whom she affectionately called "Weezy," were extremely close. They went to church together, quilted, and shopped together, and I dare say, when they were younger, they partied together. My granddad used to say, "They were two peas in a pod; why if one of them sat down on a pin, the other one would say 'Ouch!'" My grandmother had called to ask my mother to come back to Texas for a week or two, be at the funeral, and be of what help she could to my grandmother and Weezy's family.

My little brother and I were ready to go. My sister, Patsy, was more reluctant, and she was worried about missing her friends and actually started crying when Mom told her in no uncertain terms she was going with us. Patsy asked if she could walk over and tell her friend Allison she had to leave for a few weeks, and Mom told her that was a good idea.

When my sister left, my little brother and I followed on our bikes. He was still riding with training wheels, but he could hold his own. Her tears were fair game for my little brother and me. We ran around behind her, boohooing and acting like leaving our friends would ruin our lives. I would say, "Oh, what am I going to tell my friends? I will just miss them so-o-o-o much?" And then boohoo some more. My little brother would join in and repeat everything I said, and then we would both just laugh as we rode circles around her. That is until she finally picked up a rock and threw it at me. Hit me square in the mouth and knocked me off my bike. Blood and other bodily fluids shot out of my mouth along with part of my tooth.

My little brother started crying and screaming at my sister. "You kilt him, Patsy, you kilt Charles Lee. Momma's gonna murder us."

Patsy walked Jimmy and me back to the house and told us to wait in the garage while she went in and talked to Mom. "But I'm bleeding," I said.

"Oh, hush up! Your lip is a foot from your heart! I'll tell you when you can come in the house."

As my sister left, Jimmy looked at her with his deer-in-the-headlights look. The kind of look you would have if a spaceship landed in your front yard.

* * *

We began our trip two days later, after a quick visit to one of the dentists on base. Jimmy and I were still trying to figure out why Patsy did not get in trouble, but we did. We were relegated to the back seat for the entire trip. My

29

dad had bought a new Ford Fairlane, a blue and white four-door, and it was a beauty. It was our stylish conveyance back to Texas. As we set out on our journey, we were excited, but after looking at Yucca cactus, Joshua Trees, and sagebrush mile after mile, we started to get bored. My sister was poring over a magazine that looked like it was totally devoted to Elvis Presley. Patsy and Mom talked about cooking and clothes, primarily. When it came to talking about relatives, Jimmy and I would roll our eyes at each other then go back to drawing airplanes or reading comic books. Our most significant endeavor in the backseat of that Ford was trying to decide if Cisco and Pancho were murdering bad people or killing them in self-defense. It would help to remember that Jimmy was only five years old and wasn't into complex problem-solving.

Jimmy's response was, "What's the difference? They dead, right? Like Miz Weezy?"

Patsy turned around in her seat and said, "You two had better stop talking about the dead, or they will come back and get you!"

My mom said, "All of you need to quit talking about things you don't know anything about. Now is anybody in this car hungry?"

And so it went—all the way to Texas. We were so car weary when we stopped in the evenings. We couldn't wait to climb into bed and dreaded getting up in the mornings and setting out again.

We finally arrived in Tyler, Texas, three days later. When we pulled up in my grandmother's yard, she was sitting outside with my granddad and my uncles under this giant Magnolia tree. They all jumped up and came to the car and took turns hugging my mom and picking my little brother up, who never lost that struck dumb look on his face. He had not seen any of his uncles since he was a baby and didn't know what to expect. Two of my three uncles had served in WW II with my dad and then in Korea, and their idea of fun was to take their knuckles and rub your head. My other uncle, James Dalton, was just glad he wasn't on the receiving end anymore. When they got through with Jimmy, most of his hair had been rubbed off, and I swear his head was raw from the rubbing he took.

It was an East Texas rough and tumble bunch of redneck, die-hard reactionaries that made up my mom's family. They all had hearts as big as their home state. They were all well-traveled, but when they returned to the land of their birth, they reverted from the sophisticated cosmopolitan young men they had become to the boisterous provincials they once were.

After an early dinner, my grandmother announced that it was time to go to the 'Viewing.' Jimmy looked up at me and wanted to know what a viewing was. My grandmother said, "You don't need to know because you kids are staying here. This viewing is for grownups." They told my sister that she was to stay and babysit us. She looked like the dentist had just told her he was drilling. My Uncle James said, "Oh, Mama, why don't you let these kids go?"

My grandmother said, "Because I don't want any

31

incidents like what happened when they buried your Great-Granddaddy Marshall; you know when those two Fullilove boys got to wrestling around and knocked the coffin over. Y'all can just stop laughing. It was disrespectful. And old man Fullilove standing there saying, *Well, boys will be boys.* Somebody should have tanned all their hides, I'll tell you."

By now, all my uncles had joined in the conversation, along with my mom, and they were all laughing and cutting up as they reminisced about the Great Fullilove Disaster. Finally, my Uncle Ben said, "It wouldn't have been so bad if they had put pants on him."

"Well, the top part is all they usually dress up, but I bet they start putting pants on them in the future."

"I noticed you looking at him, too, Mama."

"Well, I never!" My grandmother said.

"Oh, that's okay Thelma, all anybody could talk about after Marshall rolled out of that coffin was how well-endowed he was." My granddad tried his best to console my grandmother, but he was having as much fun as his kids. "You know that runs in my family."

"I want y'all to quit this nasty talk; they's children in the room," My grandmother said. But she was trying her best to stifle a laugh.

Jimmy and I just stood there and looked from one relative to another, as they joked and laughed and brought life to that cracked linoleum-clad kitchen.

"Oh, Mama, why don't you let them go? I promise I'll look after them."

My grandmother finally capitulated. If for no other

reason than to get to the funeral home early. Louise's family wanted my grandmother to sit on a stool beside the casket and sing some of Weezy's favorite hymns and songs, which my grandmother considered the highest honor that could be bestowed on her. So my granddad piled my grandmother, my mom, my sister, and two of my uncles into his 1948 Lincoln and said he would return to pick up my Uncle James, my brother Jimmy, and me.

Jimmy and I felt like we were riding in the ultimate luxury on the way to the Burks-Walker-Tippet Funeral Home. My Uncle James asked my granddad, "Well, Dad, have you bought any insurance on this beast yet?"

"Well, I was planning on buying some today, but then Weezy died and decided to have her funeral today."

"Sure, Dad, there is always an excuse with you. One of these days, someone is gonna run into you, and you are gonna wish you had insurance."

Then, out of nowhere, another car ran a stop sign and smacked into my granddad's rear fender. Up until that moment in my life, I don't believe I had ever heard a louder sound than the sound of metal on metal. Not even Chuck Yeager breaking the sound barrier was louder than that grinding crash. Even though it was just a fender bender, and both cars were able to drive away, my uncle was relentless in poking fun at my granddad for not having insurance. My granddad got so befuddled that when he went to spit his tobacco out of the window, he forgot that the glass was rolled up.

When we finally arrived at the funeral home, my mom wanted to know why we were so late. My little brother said, "Because Granddad don't have no insurance." I thought my uncle might wet his britches.

We walked in and sat at the back. When it got to the point in the program where the preacher asked folks to line up and say their farewells to Miz Weezy, my grandmother went up and picked up her guitar and started singing 'Sweet Fern,' one of Miz Weezy's favorites. Row by row, the ushers had people stand and walk to the front to say their final goodbyes. I noticed that as people walked past my grandmother to the open casket, many of them would look back at my grandmother wide-eyed and do a double-take. When we finally reached the casket, my Uncle James held my little brother up to get a last look at Miz Weezy. First, Jimmy looked in the coffin, and then he looked at my grandmother as she started to sing, 'In the Garden,' Jimmy blurted out, "Miz Weezy is dressed just like Grandma!"

Charles Templeton is the author of the Amazon bestselling novel, *Boot: A Sorta Novel of Vietnam*. When Charles isn't busy working on his next historical fiction novel, he serves on the Board of the Writers' Colony at Dairy Hollow, a writers' retreat in Eureka Springs, Arkansas. Charles served as the Acquisitions Editor for the Colony's online literary magazine, *eMerge* from 2017 until 2022 and recently edited and published an anthology of selected works from *eMerge*, *The Dairy Hollow Echo*. More information about the author and his writing can be found at (https://www.charlestempleton.com/)

Goodbye

By

Renée Norrell

I

The year is 1962. I am eleven years old. I am leaving my grandmother, my two sisters, my cousins, my friends, my home, my school, my country, my language. I still have my parents, my little brother. And a new dress. I know what I'm leaving behind, but I have no idea what I'll get in its place. The future is still ahead of me, not only in time, but also in place. It's so strange to move forward into a fog, into the unfamiliar. But yet, I don't feel sad; maybe because I am so young, and I am not meant to hold on to a past that is still so brief.

The day of departure is here. We go to the airport, driven by an acquaintance of my father. My mother is quiet; for her this departure is most difficult. To be far away from her home, her family causes her heart to cry. But she doesn't cry; she is the one who decided that for my father to be happy and successful in life, he needed to go to a world of new opportunities, to the New World. For him she is willing to be brave, to close the curtain on her bereavement. She will make sure that he, my little brother and I see only the smile in her eyes and the determination that guides her.

Before we board the plane, one of my uncles comes to say good-bye. He is the father of a cousin my age, a friend. He is still a happy and energetic man who does not know yet of the trauma ahead of him. His daughter and a second daughter will be in a car that gets hit by a train: no survivors. For my mother the future is a haze of sadness; for my uncle sadness will define the past.

We get on the plane, a well-dressed family. My father wears a suit, as always. Only in years from now, living in the Deep South, will he abandon his jacket and tie in the hot summers. My mother looks her best with a little hat on her already gray hair. I have on my new brown woolen dress. Hubert, my five-year-old brother, is happily sporting the KLM pin he was given by a stewardess. In our seats we are ready for the long journey from Amsterdam to Toronto. Our first flight ever, so I am somewhat excited. Even the meals, which I will not await with great anticipation when I am a flight weary adult, are now a novelty, and break up the monotony of our trip. I read a bit and snooze until we reach Montreal, where we have to proceed through customs and immigration. Fortunately Pappie speaks flawless French, much appreciated by the Québécois agents. After all, it is the era of clashes in Québec between the anglo and francophone populations.

After Montreal we fly on to Toronto where Mr. Jan Heersink, the Dutch vice-Consul picks us up, and drives us to Burlington. It is dark, and I am tired, but the world around me is so alien that I do not sleep. We leave urban scenes with neon lights in all colors. We drive by my first sighting of a drive-in movie theater, and all the while Mr. Heersink, or oom Jan as I will call him later on, is talking to Pappie about the wonders of life in Canada. Fortunately he speaks in Dutch, and I think that maybe not everything will feel odd. In Burlington we first go to his house. His wife, soon to be called tante Mineke, is warm-hearted and makes me feel at home. Their four teenage sons overwhelm me, but how handsome they are! I just wish I could speak English, or they better Dutch. They are kind, but not overly interested in a shy eleven year old who can't communicate with them. I do not mind getting back in the car to be taken to the motel where we will spend the next three weeks.

Now begins one of the strangest times in my life. I feel like I'm living a life between lives; it's just not real. Not only because we're cramped into a motel room and call it home. Not only because our furniture with all my familiar things and books is still on the Atlantic. Not only because Pappie has no employment. Not only because my body is beginning to change, and I wonder if it's natural. Not only, not only, but especially because I have to go to school: a (temporary) school that is close to where a Dutch lady lives who helps me in the afternoons. A school where I am put in a class (the eighth) with kids two years older than me, just because there's a Dutch girl in that class, a girl who is not interested in me in the least. A school whose principal decides to teach me English. I go to his office, and he tries to explain the difference between the words brain and mind. The science teacher wants me to know the word snake, and tells me to point to it in a terrarium at the back of the class. I point to everything but the snake. I am stuck in a world of unfamiliar sounds, of words without meaning. I do not cry or pine for my past life as I know that I cannot go back. Nor do I look forward as I cannot imagine a house I have never seen, friends I haven't met, a language I don't understand.

I am still a child and can lose myself in some simple enjoyments of life. One of the first is Halloween. In Holland I did not know of its existence; here in Canada I quickly learn how much fun there is in running from door to door in the dark with a group of children, and being rewarded for my effort with lots of candy. With a witch's hat on my long hair I think I am someone else in a different reality. I do believe that the phrase "trick or treat" is the first one in English that I master and do not forget. I am also happy to meet a girl my own age, Annabel, who speaks both English and Dutch. She lives with her family in a house right on Lake Ontario. We are free to wander by the shore, even in the winter when much of the water is a huge frozen expanse, often covered by snow. This is also part of the new world: a climate so cold in winter that I have to get extra warm coats, boots, hats, scarves, and mittens to protect me. But I am young, and the cold doesn't bother me. One day I even skate to school over the frozen sidewalks. Unfortunately I do not know that one doesn't walk inside a building with skates on, and I am scolded by the principal. Even though Canada and Holland are both in the Western world, their cultures are different enough to cause moments of confusion, especially during this time of transition.

After a few weeks of unreal motel life, my father rents a house in Burlington. Our furniture arrives and the world is beginning to have a familiar feel to it. I don't get the cute bedroom with a window seat because it's reserved for my oldest sister Alexandra who is going to join us later. That means I have to share a room with Hubert, and it's a room with huge green vegetation designs on the wallpaper. The room is dark, but it does have a sunny alcove where I can play or read. I think the best part of this house is that I go to a different school, close by, and even though I continue in the eighth grade, I actually have a friend, Vicky, who is also a bit younger than the other kids. Some afternoons I go home with her, and we watch the *Flintstones* on her huge TV. This is how I really learn English, and also from watching the *Beverly Hillbillies*. At home we still don't have a television, and won't have one until I am in the eleventh grade, in another different world, Alabama. I like sitting in front of Vicky's TV, eating potato chips, feeling warm and cozy in what Mammie would consider to be an overheated house. This is about to change. It is now 1963. Winter is ending, as is the lack of familiarity with the English language. Pappie has accepted a position teaching Philosophy at Acadia University in Nova Scotia, and we will soon be leaving. After a little more than half a year of slowly getting settled, I will have to say "goodbye" again. To Vicky, to Annabel, to the Heersinks, to Alexandra, to Lake Ontario. To the first part of my life in Canada.

II

It's a sunny June morning. We leave early in the car

Pappie has bought just for this occasion. I'm kind of excited, as I've never been on a car trip this long. Even being in the back with an obnoxious little brother is bearable as long as he leaves me alone. I love feeling the wind in my hair streaming through the open window. Somehow I feel free and happy with anticipation. We cross the border into the United States, a country I have only seen across Niagara Falls, and that was in the winter when all I saw was ice. Pappie drives through upper New York State on the wonderful expanse of endless highway, takes a wrong exit, and ends up having to add 100 miles to our journey. Mammie has no criticism, as she also, is approaching this move with a sense of optimism. Pappie finally has a job ahead of him, and he's bought a house that has been renovated just for us. Maybe this Canadian adventure, the uprooting of the family will be successful and will erase years of worries. Maybe it will lead to stability, to new friendships, and ultimately to frequent trips back to Holland. Maybe ... maybe.

We spend the night in Saint John, New Brunswick, as we are to take the ferry across to Digby the next morning. The hotel is quaint, looking out over the harbor, and the ferry is a novel experience. Standing on the deck during the crossing over the Bay of Fundy, I feel like an adventurer. Nova Scotia appears quickly under a grey sky. Hues of green surround the town where we dock and fill the air with freshness. The drive to Wolfville, the town where Acadia University is located, only takes a couple of hours, and soon we are welcomed most kindly by the people who will host us until our furniture arrives.

There's even a girl, a bit younger than myself who takes it upon herself to erase feelings of strangeness before they occur. Smiles preempt tears; laughter and conversation fill voids of loneliness.

Furniture arrives and we finally settle in a renovated house on a lovely, quiet street. I have my own room this time, across the hall upstairs from Arnaudine (my sister, six years older than me), who has come to join us after finishing her Gymnasium final exams in Holland. The wood floors are new, light in color, and impart a feeling of cheeriness. Downstairs, I really love the little alcove in the hall where I can sit and read, looking out of the window or into the living room which has glass-paneled doors to keep out the cold from the front door. Instead of a dining room we have a piano room, but the kitchen has a breakfast bar. It's in that house that we begin to often eat our evening meal in the living room. Cozier, and a good place for conversation because we still don't have a television. I like the house, also the garage where we set up the Ping-Pong table as Pappie sells his car soon after arriving in Nova Scotia. Apparently the renovations to the house were more costly than expected, and walking is not a problem. Only for getting groceries does Mammie have to use a taxi. My walking has increased as I get a dog— my own dog!

Dingo is a six month old border collie, black and brown and white. He is super furry, super huggable, a great friend. Well, he is my friend, not the friend of the old people in the house down the street. He chases their cat right into their house, and manages to get a scratched eye for his boldness. He is also not the friend of a bulldog who lives a couple of streets away, who attacks him one day, and has to be kicked by a boy wearing steel toed boots to get him to turn loose of Dingo's leg. Dingo is such a friend that I will protect him from anything and anybody. One afternoon Mammie is sleeping upstairs, ill with one of her frequent migraines. Dingo starts to go up the stairs, but doesn't get far because Pappie pulls him down by his tail. I am furious and hit Pappie on his back. Pappie turns around with cold, angry eyes. I run away; Dingo is unperturbed.

Summer time does not last forever, so I must go to my new school. The principal is wise and suggests that I repeat the eighth grade as I am so young, even then one year younger than classmates. Mammie and Pappie agree, and what a great decision that turns out to be. The class is small and all are friendly, including the teachers. I don't feel like an outsider. I participate in after-school sports such as swimming, volleyball, track and field, and even become a cheerleader. With a group of classmates I go on hikes, bicycle adventures into rural Nova Scotia (yes, in those days it's still safe to be unaccompanied by adults), play tennis, go to the movies, have parties (Beatle lip sync fests!), go sledding, ice-skating. We go to basketball games at the university. I get to sing in a televised talent show. I have my first boyfriend. And my second boyfriend. And a third boyfriend. Clouds that appear from time to time leave no mark.

Then the moment of saying goodbye comes back. Pappie needs to find a new job, and, after many trips to the post office to send his résumés, and a trip to the US for interviews, he gets a position at Alabama College in Montevallo, Alabama. My school friends tell me about racial violence in nearby Birmingham, and warn me to get a gun. I find all this hard to believe, but am unhappy that I'll have to leave a place of comfort and friendship. The house is now empty of furniture, the perfect place for one last party. All my friends come, even a boyfriend who lives across Nova Scotia, on the Atlantic Ocean. We laugh, eat, and dance, and then shut the door forever.

III

Our path to Montevallo takes a long time as we first take a ship back to Holland, by way of England, the first time since our emigration, so very long ago, or so it seems. For Mammie this is a going home moment. For Pappie there is anxiety about his new job, but, fortunately also pleasure in seeing some old friends and playing on beautiful, old Dutch organs. For me there's fun: cousins, my best friend, a loving grandmother, Alexandra, aunts and uncles, all make sure that I don't get bored. I have my first glass of champagne, my first gin and tonic, my first cigarette. Oh, I am so grownup! But, of course, time dictates that we must leave, and once again we get on an airplane, more than one, and land in Birmingham on July 4, 1966.

A day I'll never forget; it is hot, so hot that I think the airplane's engines must be heating the tarmac. And, how strange, the lady who picks us up from the airport, the wife of the Dean at the college, speaks English, but with an accent which sounds so foreign. Later I learn that this is Southern, not Alabama Southern, but Virginia

43

Southern. On the road to Montevallo there are strange sights: red clay and kudzu. A day later I see another oddity, one that I will never get used to: roaches! We have a house belonging to the College awaiting us, but our furniture is not to be expected for another few weeks, so off we go to a local motel, the Clara Neal in Calera. Fortunately, there's a swimming pool and the motel owners have a daughter who befriends me. On Friday evenings, Pappie drives her and me to the armory where I mingle with the local boys on the dance floor. I have fun but the rural surroundings and people make me feel as though I am living in a different universe.

When we finally move into the house in Montevallo, and I meet some kids from the town, a sense of normalcy returns. With a group organized by the Methodist Church, I go to Lake Junalaska in North Carolina for a week. There is, of course, some bible study, but mostly we are allowed to explore the lake and do what we want as long as it's with others. A perfect introduction to new friendships that pave the way to acceptance once I start school in September. I adapt easily: classmates are friendly and much intrigued by this girl who dares to wear miniskirts to school. I quickly become a football player's girlfriend, and football is much revered in the South. The principal likes me; he lets me substitute Canadian history as a requirement for graduation instead of the prescribed class in Alabama history. And I get another dog, this time a German Shepherd puppy that I name Bodo after a medieval Dutch knight. Time passes: I graduate from high school; I go to college and dream of becoming a famous

44

opera singer; I get married; I go to Graduate School and earn my PhD in French; I travel; I start teaching at a small liberal arts college in Birmingham; I have a child; the child earns his PhD in physics; the child gets married; the child finds a job with the Federal government; the child moves to Washington, D.C.; the child has children. Life follows predictable patterns.

My story jumps many years into the future to pick up an old theme. My parents get old, very old, and depend on me. I spend much time and energy to take care of them, and in return feel much love, for them, and from them. When they finally depart, Pappie first, at age 100, and then Mammie two years later, at age 96, the goodbyes empty the world. I am not sure of the direction, the substance of my life. Memories must guide me, but at the same time I must look forward and find another path.

IV

For a couple of years I can make no decisions, but with husband Fred's encouragement and help, I decide that another goodbye will be necessary. Fred and I decide to help our son, Hans and his wife, Laura with the children by moving close by to them. It's a decision that many grandparents have made before us, but that doesn't necessarily make it an easy one. Of course, we are so happy to be involved in our grandchildren's lives, to feel useful and to create a real bond of the heart. Seeing Hans often, and speaking Dutch with him provides a continuity of the essence of who I am, of the culture I was born into. Leaving a house, however, where I lived over 30 years, leaving a state where I lived ever since my immigration to the US, leaving friends, and also leaving the last place where I was with Mammie and Pappie makes me feel uprooted. Our new abode has our old furniture, and most important, my piano (I always said that I wouldn't leave without it, even if it meant strapping it to my back), but it's not home. I have to work at making my imprint on my surroundings, and to have them be imprinted on me. I walk a lot because if I see a place through car windows, and pass through it quickly, I cannot feel connections. I also meet a friend-to-be who was born in Alabama, and is a pianist! She and I start to play duets, which, unfortunately, we have to pause because of a pandemic that interrupts many normal activities. Fortunately, I get together with her for wine time at the picnic table outside of our condo many a Saturday, and get to know her. I also keep in touch with my old friends by calling them often on the phone; hearing their voices regularly fills the distances between us and creates closeness. "Goodbye" becomes a weekly "au revoir."

V

The final section of my life with the final goodbye remains to be written. It is one that everybody would like to read, or write, but nobody will. So I shall close with an imagined ending.

At night, goodbye day;
In dreams I create a world;
I will be my dream.

Renée Norrell earned her PhD in French at the University of Alabama and taught French language, literature, and culture for thirty years at Birmingham-Southern College. She now lives with her husband Fred in Virginia where she spends much of her time taking care of grandchildren, playing the piano, learning Spanish, walking, and writing haikus.

Welcome Home

By

Ellaraine Lockie

I return from Kenya to find the living room redecorated
Two twin beds disguised as sofas
lounge in the center of the room
To accommodate the grandsons he says
Off to one side an altar of toy trucks
baseballs and bats, scooters, video
and board games invite me to play
Harley Davidson books litter the coffee table

Dining room walls display Jimmy Buffet and ski travel
posters
A mini IMAX screen cemented to the ESPN channel
ovals around a pool table that replaces the dining table
Cheeseburger in Paradise oozes from speakers

The kitchen counter has been transformed
into a tropical themed bar with Barbie doll
sized pastel umbrellas in a glass
Cigars in another
Black enamel painted cupboards
hide chips, nuts and Margarita mixes
Refrigerator, a case of Coors
and leftover Arby's take-out
Model airplanes hang in hallways
Big-boy league baseball trophies

share shelf space with team photos
A new trombone case leans against a corner

His mistress stands in the bedroom
shaped in of a bag of golf clubs
holding what looks like Ben Wah balls
and little stilettoed plastic sticks
Stuffed parrots strut over the top half of the bed

Designer colognes fill the medicine chest
The toilet plays the San Francisco Giants'
fight song when flushed
I sit down on the bed and see the backyard
gentrified into a putting range
Complete with sand dunes and fish pond

I pick up a parrot-shaped telephone
to make a joint therapy appointment
Jump when I lie back and see my reflection
on the mirrored ceiling
I wake up and say hello to another day
with a newly retired spouse

Mother of Trees
--After The Hidden Life of Trees by Peter Wohlleben

By

Ellaraine Lockie

You don't mention to the mostly multilingual neighbors
that although you can't speak their languages
you understand that of trees
How you feel the ultrasonic screams as one
of those neighbors hacks down a healthy pine tree
A little each day like Hannibal Lecter would
until a concrete driveway deadens its SOS

How a chainsaw severs dreams at night
after the sweet gums gracing the sidewalk
are reduced to stumps
The word *messy*, one that nuthatches

chickadees and finches can't fathom
The same trees that beckoned you
on morning walks to tear ivy off their barks
Patting them as a mother would her injured child

The apricot tree that fed
the cul-de-sac jam for thirty years
Slain, by new owners who wanted
nothing alive in their front yard
You shudder to think what they did
with the dwarf orange you gave them

as a housewarming gift

Then there's the neighbor who butchered
your own 40-year oak grove when you were gone
so he could have more sunlight
Squirrels deprived of acorns
Nests naked to predators
You stripped of privacy, shade and serenity

Guardian Angel

By

Ellaraine Lockie

It wasn't Wonder Woman's shield
that stopped the South African rhino's charge
So close the woman in the open jeep
inhaled the exhaled stench
Nor zap from Batman's batarang that paralyzed
the pack of wild dogs slobbering
over her fetal curl in the Bali meadow
It wasn't the Maasai god Ngai who flipped
the Kenya aircraft right-side-up seconds before landing

Not for this woman whose six-year-old self
sat on her Uncle Hank's lap in his prairie cabin
When he outlined how he'd watch over, keep her safe
Wait for her on the other side, as timeless
as the crucifix on the wall witnessing the covenant

A pact she still carries around like a security blanket
decades later knowing it can foster even the smallest
whim
The eggs from a neighbor who is leaving on vacation
just when our woman is two short for a soufflé
A grasshopper on her California screen door in mid-
winter
after she writes a poem of longing for their song
So on this summer's Montana prairie walk

after she complains in public of no wild flax
to plunge into paper pulp
The next morning the woman isn't surprised
to find by the cabin a bush of it ablaze in blossoms

With the reverence of an altar boy
she presses each long-legged beauty
in its blue floral hat onto a phone book page
Before closing the book to hear it sizzle
like an electric wall socket gone haywire

The heart-stopping jolt enflames the woman
who becomes an instant believer
in séances, Ouija boards and second comings
Until the young honey bee crawls out of the book
like a superhero in the insect world

The woman's superhero remains as quiet
as the sun that sets oblivious of continent
The woman as sure it will rise the next morning
as she is secure in the safety of her next trip to Africa

Ellaraine Lockie's recent work has won the Oprelle
Publishing's Poetry Masters Contest, Poetry Super Highway
Contest, the Nebraska Writers Guild's Women of the Fur Trade
Poetry Contest and New Millennium's Monthly Musepaper
Poetry Contest. Chapbook collections have won Poetry
Forum's Chapbook Contest Prize, San Gabriel Valley Poetry
Festival Chapbook Competition, Encircle Publications
Chapbook Contest, Best Individual Poetry Collection Award
from Purple Patch , and The Aurorean's Chapbook Choice
Award. Ellaraine is Poetry Editor for the lifestyles magazine,
LILIPOH.

Nguyen Van Tien & Family

By

Larry Laverentz

In August of 1975, Nguyen Van Tien and his twelve family members were sponsored by my family. They were among the 125,000 or so that had escaped from Vietnam immediately prior to the fall of South Vietnam's government in April of 1975. When I was in Vietnam in the 1960s, Captain Tien was the district chief of Du Long, one of four districts in Ninh Thuan Province. With the fall of Saigon and the emergence of refugees, Melody and I had submitted documentation to the Department of State agreeing to sponsor families of people with whom I had worked or knew. Tien and his family were among these.

The story of the Tien's family escape from Vietnam in 1975 has similarities to the later escape of many Vietnamese in the late 1970s and early 1980s. Among the innumerable incidents were harrowing escapes and crowded boats some of which sank in the South China Sea. Others were fortunate enough to be picked up by American and other ships while others made it to the shores of Thailand, Malaysia or the Philippines. At the time of South Vietnam's fall, Tien was Lieutenant Colonel Tien, Deputy Chief for Security in Ninh Thuan Province. His wife, with their ten children, ranging in age from two to twenty, and Tien's father left the province early and moved on foot the more than 100 miles from Phan Rang, the province capital, to Saigon. According to the stories they told, they hid mostly during the day and traveled at night amidst weapons fire and other noises. Because the family had a relative that worked in the American Embassy they were able to obtain passes to enter an area to board a helicopter and leave Vietnam.

Lieutenant Colonel Tien, in true unselfish fashion and at the risk of his own life, stayed in Phan Rang until the day before it fell to the North Vietnamese Army. Because he had made previous arrangements, he was able to be flown to Saigon on an L 19 spotter plane. By the time he was able to reach the American Embassy his contact had already departed, and he was therefore unable to get a pass. He then went to one of the departure locations at Tan Son Nhut Airport where he found heavily barbed concertina wire surrounding the departure area. Tien said he purchased a pair of pliers from a young boy for roughly $5.00 and was able to cut his way through the wire and get onto a helicopter and eventually to Wake Island, one of two places along with Guam, to which the Vietnamese were being shuttled.

Wake Island had tens of thousands of refugees living there in camps. His family had obviously not heard from him and had no way of knowing his status. It was an emotional reunion when by chance they met. They left Wake Island and were taken to Indiantown Gap, an army base in Pennsylvania, one of four military camps Vietnamese were sent to until they could be permanently resettled. As described in the Marvin and Mary Margaret

Greenawalt chapter, I worked at the camp at Fort Chaffee in Fort Smith, Arkansas for the first fifteen days of persons arriving from Wake or Guam. The stories were similar for all arrivals. They had lost their country, their familiar surroundings and their sense of pride and dignity.

In August of 1975, Melody, Eric, Marni and I lived on eighty acres east of McLouth (Kansas). We had prepared for their arrival by putting all of our beds in the master bedroom and borrowing cots for Tien's family to sleep on in the other two bedrooms and the family room. Upon arrival, we showed them where they would be sleeping and Tien walked into our two car garage and said, "What is wrong with this?" Our response was something like: "It is a garage, dirty, etc." He essentially pschawed it and said, "We will stay here." They immediately proceeded to rearrange and clean the garage and this is where they slept.

The four or five weeks the Tien family stayed with us was a meaningful and educational experience for my family. The three older children, all girls, Huong, Thu and Tam, stayed with Gary Sullivan, a former fraternity brother of mine, and his wife and two daughters in Topeka. The remainder of the family lived with us. We were helped with supplies and support by other people in the community. This effort was led by Mrs. Snook, the wife of Dr. Snook, McLouth's only physician.

Melody tells a story about the occasion when Mrs. Tien lined up her seven younger kids and told them to put out their hands, palms down. She slapped each one of them for not watching four-year-old Eric more closely. He had jumped off the bar in the tiled family room and although unhurt, she had admonished them. Mrs. Tien and her children made every effort to minimize the work of Melody by virtue of her family's cleaning, cooking and performing other chores.

In less than a week after arrival, I drove Tien into Kansas City to look for work. This former Lieutenant Colonel ended up shortly thereafter getting a job as an apprentice baker for the Forum Cafeteria. On one occasion we drove through Leavenworth on the way home to pick up a fifty pound bag of rice. After getting the rice I turned off Highway 7 onto Country Club Road and asked Tien if he wanted to drive. Somewhat surprised he accepted my offer and got into the driver's seat. I began messing with the radio because the Royals were playing in Baltimore. I looked up and he was going about 50 MPH in a 35 MPH zone. About that time, we passed a crossroad where a City of Leavenworth patrol car was sitting. The patrol car pulled out behind us, and I finally got Tien to understand to pull off to the side of the road and stop. The officer came to the driver's side and asked Tien to see his driver's license. I immediately spoke up by saying that he did not have a driver's license yet because he had just arrived from Vietnam. The officer asked us to step out and move to the back of the car. After a little more conversation, he turned to Tien, reached out his hand and said, "Welcome to this country." He then turned to me and said, "You are a gentleman." The only thing I could think to say was, "You are a gentleman too." We drove home without a ticket.

In order to get Tien to the location for bakery training by 7:00, I was getting up early and driving him there and then going to work at the federal building on 12th Street by 7:00 a.m. I would pick him up after work and return home. After a couple of weeks we were able to find a rental house not far from Rockhurst College. More time was consumed from leaving and getting home because of the need to drive to his new home twice a day. Thankfully, I was able to get a person from my office to begin sharing this responsibility. I recognized that getting him a driver's license was imperative, but thought that should not be problem because Tien had driven an army jeep in Vietnam Getting him to pass the driving part of the driver's test became a challenging experience. Not until the fifth try was he able to get a license. The first time I drove up to the testing place on 13th Street across from the federal building. I turned the car off and Tien moved to the driver's side with the examiner in the passenger seat. I was standing on the sidewalk watching and listening. The examiner said, "Okay, start the car." Tien did not know how to start it, because I had always driven and then turned it over to him without turning off the ignition. They went no further, and the examiner answered my pleading question by saying, "I can hardly pass him if he cannot start the car." The next week we had the same examiner again. They were able to leave but returned in about two minutes. Upon asking, why the quick return, the tester said, "Well he made a right turn from the middle lane." His third try resulted in a similar experience. I decided we needed to get to a friendlier and less busy place for his testing. The fourth testing place was in Raytown where the driver's license bureau was in a smaller shopping center. I watched Tien and the examiner as they drove off from the front of the license bureau office. They drove around a part of the parking lot and immediately returned to the starting point. The examiner answered my somewhat emotional question by saying that he had pulled out in front of someone by not yielding to the right. As I drove back to his home, I made some kind of irrational statement like, "You are going to kill me with not being able to get a license and my long hours of driving." We went back to his home, and I called the Sears Driving School. On Monday of the next week, I picked him up and asked him to drive. I could tell a difference almost immediately with the thought in the back of my head that I was not a good teacher. Shortly thereafter we drove to the license bureau in Grandview because I had been told this was a good place to get tested. Tien passed the test. In the interim he had purchased a car and had significantly increased his degree of independence.

My family and I had other experiences, most of them positive and enlightening. I had taken Tien to a bank to open a checking account. Two or three weeks later I asked to look at his checkbook. Somewhat self-righteously, I said, "You only have deposits in your register; you have to also record the checks you write." His response was: "I have not written any checks." When I asked how this could be, he said his three older girls were giving one-half of their money from their jobs busing tables at Crown Center for family use.

It must have been seven or eight months later that the Tien's were able to purchase a house in midtown Kansas City. My family and I would try to visit them every two weeks or so. We were always treated to lots of attention and a big meal. During this time, Mrs. Tien and her kids starting making Vietnamese egg rolls (cha gio) for a restaurant. She would line up their kids in assembly line fashion with each one obviously having an assigned responsibility. When we visited, each of Tien's children might have one toy. Our two kids, despite having a crowd of toys at home, were usually enamored with these and the Tien's would say: "It is okay; they can have it." There were no objections from his kids. We would say: "No, they have plenty of toys at home."

One Sunday when we went there, a previous employee of Tien in Vietnam, former Lieutenant Lam, was visiting with his family on their way moving from Ohio to California. It was on that occasion that Lam told me about his younger sister Phuong and her death. The information was sobering and brought back a flood of memories, along with some "what ifs."

Captain Tien's District in Ninh Thuan, Du Long, was the least populated of the four districts. Approximately one-half of the hamlets were inhabited by Montagnards. As district chief, Tien was responsible for the hamlets within the village structure in his district. Each village would have about six hamlets; and even though hamlet chiefs were elected, the village, also with a chief, was really the local government. Tien had about a company of popular or local forces (troops) stationed at his headquarters.

Each hamlet also had its own popular forces troops. Tien was also responsible for assisting and monitoring the implementation of self-help projects in his district. It was probably every two or three years that a hamlet could choose a self-help project. A project could be a market place, irrigation project, health facility or some other activity that was supposed to have been chosen by the people in the hamlet. As the title implies, the local inhabitants were expected to provide the labor. There was also a separate school construction program for which my office provided building materials as well. It seems a school would otherwise cost about 40.000 piastres or about $400. The district office also had administrative responsibilities within the province structure.

Although I had a good relationship with all four district chiefs, I considered Tien to be the most progressive. He was the district chief that asked me if I would be willing to have a Montagnard boy, Mang Don, live with me and go to high school. Tien and I would occasionally go up the road to Trai Ca (translation fish camp) and have lunch. This was my introduction and only occasions with respect to eating raw fish.

Tien and his siblings and parents, along with his wife before their marriage, had moved from North Vietnam after the fall of Dien Bien Phu and the Geneva Agreement in 1954. Approximately, a million Vietnamese made the trip from the North to the South.

A little more than twenty years ago the Tien family

moved from Kansas City to Houston. Their second daughter was living there with her husband and his family. By the time they moved their first and third daughters had also married. Each of the three daughters was married in the Catholic Church on Campbell Street in the Northeast area of Kansas City. We were invited to the weddings as well as to the big and festive dinners that followed. Members of the family always treated us like royalty. Several of the younger children obtained degrees to include one becoming a dentist, another an engineer. I am sorry and embarrassed, and even ashamed, that we did not stay in touch with members of the family and now have no contact with them.

Nguyen Van Tien along with his wife and family had gone through difficult and challenging times that are hard for us to understand or fully appreciate. He was forced to uproot his life twice, the first time with his parents and siblings. Despite the difficult happenings in their lives, I detected no sign of bitterness, only resilience and a dedication to achieving happy and successful lives. They lived their Christian faiths from being a part of the Catholic Church. The grace and generosity of the Tien family were astonishing and far outweighed the support of our family for them. As a family, like millions of other refugees from Southeast Asia, they made us better as a nation.

Larry Laverentz, *The Not So Ordinary People on the Roads I've Traveled*, Chapter 32. P. 247 Cahaba Press, 2020.

A Refugee Experience

By

Larry Laverentz

Oh, it is quiet now
But there is no peace
My tears are gone
But there is no release.

What is my fate?
To live…yet die
What can sustain me?
No more tears to cry!

My children are laughing
Embers rise from the fire
The closeness of my people
Only that do I desire.

The quiet is broken
Death approaches it seems
I cry out in anguish
It's another of my dreams.

There is my home!
Sun baked yard, staked fence
Trees swaying in the breeze
Life holds no suspense!

I walk to the door

Then my thoughts become blurred
I awake from my slumber
And remember what has occurred.

My soul feels empty
I long for what was
Have I no control
If not me…who does?

My children are sleeping nearby
Their dreams…different from mine
I see peace on their faces
Hope and love they combine.

My children are with me
Though my life is not whole
I am now healing
Peace now comes to my soul.

Larry Laverentz grew up on a cattle feeding and crop farm in Northeast Kansas. After graduating from Kansas State University with a degree in Agricultural Economics, he worked as an agricultural volunteer in Vietnam between 1961 and 1963 with International Voluntary Services, the organization the Peace Corps was patterned after. In 1964 he joined the U.S. Agency for International Development and served for three plus years as the senior civilian adviser to the Ninh Thuan Province Chief in the U.S. support of the Vietnamese Pacification Program. Subsequently, he held various positions for twenty years in federal programs, including refugee resettlement and other social service areas in the Kansas City regional office of the Department of Health and Human Services. He holds a Master's of Public Administration from the University of Pittsburgh.

It Had To Be You

By

Milton P. Ehrlich

The beginning of November
reminds me of Kristallnacht
as the last of leaves drenched
in gold flash against the sky.
I can still smell the smoke of
burning books as you appear
dressed in an outfit you saved
for my funeral.
You say: *There's nothin to it,
as Jim Creed used to announce
after solving an insurmountable
problem.*
Suddenly, you vanish … and I'm
left wondering if I just had
a hypnagogic hallucination
or did you just pay me a visit?
It had to be you. Wonderful you.
It had to be you.

Waiting

By

Milton P. Ehrlich

I search the sky for airplanes,
hoping you will leave a plane
and fly down with your wings
so we can be together again
with my arms all around you
draped in gold and silver robes
with the taste of Piper-Heidsieck
on our tongues.
The stars in your eyes will shine
a light for me to find you in the
hidden world of shadowland.
We'll never say goodbye again.
Moments before you died—
you uttered: *I will wait for you.*

Milton P. Ehrlich Ph.D. is a 90-year-old psychologist and a veteran of the Korean War. He has published many poems in periodicals such as the *London Grip, Arc Poetry Magazine, Descant Literary Magazine, Wisconsin Review, Red Wheelbarrow, Christian Science Monitor,* and the *New York Times.*

(https://emerge-writerscolony.org/author/Milton/)

The Tailor Shop

By

Don Soderberg

At certain times, such as now, I open a file to scan the record of an event involving me that occurred some years ago. At first it seemed merely a dreamy little story born of an active subconscious mind. But it soon became sufficiently significant that preserving the memory in written word seemed important. And, eventually, the memory deserved to be named, as you can see below.

* * *

The trolley moved along the grassy median that split St Charles Avenue from Canal Street all the way uptown past the universities and Audubon Park. It clattered to a stop in an old business district two blocks short of Canal Street.

I watched as a young man stepped from the trolley to the grass below and stood waiting in the gray rain for the trolley car to move on. This certainly wasn't an elegant part of the city, just old brick buildings opening to quaint shops with occasional lobby entrances to offices above. Searching for his destination, he spotted a sign for the tailor shop. Heading that way, he stepped over the trolley tracks and walked across the street trying to avoid the larger puddles along the way.

Oddly, the tailor shop was below ground level, entered by descending a worn stairwell, guarded on the sidewalk above by a black iron railing to prevent any distracted pedestrians from stumbling below. The man thought how unlikely it was to find any shop below street level in a city that sits ten feet below sea level. But dreams make their own reality, and there it was, with the stairway dimly lit by light from the shop below.

Watching the man start down the stairway, my perspective began to shift. Nearing the bottom of the steps, I realized the man in the dream was actually me, and I was about to become more an active participant than observer in this dreamy story. Shaking the rain from my coat, I entered the shop where my presence was announced by the tinkle of bells hung on the top of the door. I found myself in a compact space dominated by a large cutting table in the center of the room strewn with a variety of fabrics. Bolts of cloth were shelved along one wall with a rack of finished dresses and suits on the opposite side of the shop.

The bells had barely stopped ringing when I heard laughter and the curtains covering the door to a back room parted to admit two young women, laughing and chattering between themselves as though some private joke had just occurred. In spite of the ringing door bells, they seemed surprised to see a man actually standing there in the shop, but they quickly recovered to greet me.

In unison the two said, "You must be here to pick up the suit you ordered." Not waiting for a response, they went to the rack of finished suits and began to carefully examine tickets attached to the items hanging there. After some apparent confusion, they finally plucked a suit from the rack, brought it over and urged me to try it on.

Stepping from the dressing room, I had to admit the suit fit me quite well. But the fabric was an outlandish plaid: woven in orange and yellow and brown with a touch of red here and there. It looked like something a clown would wear around a circus. Speechless, I could not believe this was a suit I had actually ordered.

At this point, I became the center of attention, while the role the chattering duo was to play in this little drama became more apparent. The two women, one blond, one brunette, wore dresses strategically cut to exhibit their substantial cleavage, now vigorously displayed, and designed to hint at what might lie beyond. The two clearly intended to distract me from any logical complaint I might want to make about the clownish suit at that moment. Chattering and flirting incessantly, they assured me the suit fit so beautifully and that I would surely come to appreciate it, as they did.

And then, once more the curtains to the back room parted and a small balding man with wire rim spectacles entered the shop. His white shirt sleeves were rolled up and a measuring tape hung around his neck. Here was the tailor himself. He scowled at the women and admonished them to be quiet.

Turning to me still in the plaid suit, the tailor said, "Don't be annoyed with these two; they mean well and are very good at what they do. Still, they can be very distracting. But they are correct; that suit fits you very well. I don't think any adjustments are necessary."

Dreamily, I watched myself in a stumbling attempt to express my doubts about the clownish plaid suit, but the wise little tailor was well ahead of me.

"You came to us," the tailor said, "asking for three suits that would fit you well and reflect your position in life over time. If you think about your life today, I believe you'll realize that suit fits you perfectly. And I'm sure the next suit will also serve you well when you are ready for it."

At that point the women began to whisper to each other, and finally asked the tailor if they might show me the fabric chosen for my second suit. Following a moment of hesitation, the tailor agreed, and the women pulled a bolt of rich woolen fabric from the shelves. The cloth was dark blue with a very light gray pinstripe, something a banker or financial manager might wear. All in all, it suggested a successful life. The tailor stroked the fabric gently while explaining he clearly saw a much different life in my future, though it would be some years before that would happen.

Chattering again, the women asked the tailor if they might bring out the fabric for my third suit. With no hesitation this time the tailor replied, "I don't yet know what that fabric will be, and our guest is a long way from being ready for it."

The tailor made no promise of when the second suit would be ready, much less the third, but assured me the suits would be ready when needed.

So, in a moment of doubt, but resignation, I changed

again. The plaid suit was hung on a hanger and covered for me to carry into the rainy afternoon outside. Then I see myself leaving the underground tailor shop, climbing the stairs back to street level, and waiting for the uptown trolley to take me home, as the dream fades to an end.

I rarely retained any vivid memory of my dreams. But this one would be different. Over the next two weeks this dream was twice played again in my sleep. Each exactly as it was the first time.

By the third occurrence of the dream, I began to realize there must be something subtle, but powerful and significant, about this dreamy trip to the tailor shop that I was not comprehending at that moment. It seemed as though some librarian in the subconscious insisted this dream be remembered and stored someplace where, in a fully conscious state, I could recall and relive the story. The whole experience seemed to take on the character of a vision rather than an ordinary, if perplexing, dream. But, to what end?

Clearly, this dream spoke to some aspect of me, or my personality that normally resides deep in the background of my mind, some place where one questions the course of one's life or purpose.

Looking back over nearly fifty years, I can still clearly recall the tailor shop and the words of the tailor whose assessments have proven to be quite accurate.

At the time of the dream my life did resemble a three-ring circus: a young father; Army officer; and graduate student, embracing a new world of economics, game theory, statistical decision theory, operations research, and just plain living. All in the alien world of New Orleans.

That craziness would persist for nearly two decades. First, with ten years in the Army Medical Service Corps. There were official job descriptions; but, apart from them, I was once told by a senior official that my responsibilities would simply include lots of things. That was clearly the best job description I have ever received. Those years were filled by various roles in hospital management and a tour of duty shoveling money at the Pentagon. Then several more clownish years of steps and missteps before eventually transitioning into two decades of blue suit attire with steady roles in finance and corporate management.

I'm not sure when the clownish plaid suit found itself retired and pushed to the back of the closet; I guess it happened gradually with less and less use over time. But at some point, the blue suit was being more appropriately used on a regular basis. The tailor had delivered as promised, but I can't recall exactly when that dark blue pinstripe suit was delivered. There were still missteps, but life generally settled down to accepted responsibilities and a measure of financial comfort. Then again, after some time, the blue suit itself rarely left the closet, and I would occasionally be asked if a third suit had yet been delivered from the tailor shop. But a third suit was never forthcoming, and I finally gave up ever expecting it.

Yet some aspects of the dreamy tailor shop have persisted almost daily over all this time. Some parts of dreams may be obvious at the time, but their significance is only realized over a longer time frame: such is the relevance of the two women in the tailor shop. At the time they were dressed and acting in a manner to gain my attention while distracting me from the moment and adding uncertainty to the little drama. As with most aspects of the visit to the tailor shop, they would turn out to be emblematic of much more. In reality they were representative of the two dominant distracting relationships of my life. First, a blond for over two decades in which we raised kids, became older, and grew to be too different from each other. And then a brunette who after thirty plus years of marriage still distracts me in the best of ways with welcome regularity.

Now, fifty years after that first dream of a trip to a tailor shop on a rainy day in New Orleans, I'm a decade into retirement. It has been time spent trying to satisfy a boundless curiosity and, in some respects, to reinvent myself. And today I am pretty comfortable in my own skin just as it is, and I no longer expect to hear from the little tailor.

Though on occasion, I go to bed wondering if tonight I might dream well and have a chance to visit the tailor shop once again. I expect the shop itself, sitting below street level, will look very much as it did before. It has probably aged a bit, as we all have. But somehow I expect the tailor himself will be largely unchanged over all these years. I can envision him in the same wire rim glasses, with his shirt sleeves rolled up, and an old tailor's tape hanging about his neck, perhaps to measure time as much as cloth.

It's not that I any longer have concerns about the suits. I would just like to see him. He would probably have a welcoming smile and make me feel comfortable to be back in his shop.

A quizzical look from me might bring a wry smile to his face and a twinkle in his eye and cause him to say, "You look fine in the suit you're wearing today. As you have learned, a tailor like me can only shape so much of a life for you. The truth is that ultimately each of us has to take what is given them and weave the fabric of their own life. It certainly took you long enough, but I am pleased that you finally figured it out."

I can't envision much I could say, or would want to say to the little tailor, beyond the opportunity to quietly let my face show my appreciation for life's lessons.

This dream has been with me for so long, I find it hard to believe the little drama with the tailor shop is completely finished. So, I'll still sleep and dream and hope to visit the tailor in his shop again; just to thank him … maybe tonight.

Donald N. Soderberg was born in South Bend, Indiana. His formal education included Purdue, Notre Dame, and Tulane Universities, culminating with a Ph.D. in Management Science from Tulane. His career included work in academic and business organizations, principally in operations and finance. Retiring as CEO of Illinois Graphics in 2010, he moved to the Ozarks. Now he regularly feeds his curiosity and tries to reinvent himself in Northwest Arkansas where he lives with Mariellen Griffith, his wife of thirty years.

Once Upon A Time

By

Mariellen Griffith

Once upon a time—isn't that how stories begin? It worked for fairy tales, why not modern tales?

I had an experience that may sound like a fairy tale. As I look back at that experience, I wonder if it was a dream. The experience was out of the ordinary. Some people would say: 'You experienced your second sight, or...you stepped into another dimension.' I have no rational explanation; all I can tell you is that I had an extraordinary experience.

Before reading my story, I must ask you, 'Do you believe in the world of fairies and angels, elves, and garden spirits? Are you familiar with Shakespeare's two plays, *A Mid-Summer Night's Dream* and *The Tempest?*' Fairies play a major part in the plays. If you have read these plays or read stories of humans stepping into a fairy circle, or like Rip Van Winkle, meeting strange men in the Catskill Mountains, drinking with them and falling asleep for twenty years, you may believe my story.

However, I didn't step into a fairy circle or get drunk with men in the mountains and fall asleep for twenty

79

years. My story is different. Once upon a time, many years ago, and for many years thereafter, gardening has been my love and creative endeavor. I experienced the love of gardening from my parents. As a child, I watched my parents plant and work in a large vegetable garden. My mother also loved landscaping the yard. She planted shrubs and trees. As a child, I was asked to pull weeds in the garden or pick strawberries. I didn't like that kind of gardening. I preferred reading books of fairy stories in the house. I have always wanted to see fairies. One story that I read was about young girls in England during the Victorian Period seeing fairies and photographing them. Colonel Doyle, author of the Sherlock Holmes stories, heard these stories and believed them. Maybe fairies are real.

One early May morning, after working for several hours in my present garden, I sat down on a butterfly shaped steel bench near the waterfall and small pond that I had created. As I looked over the garden, I became aware of the sweet smell of a red rose bush nearby. Overhead, I heard the buzzing of bees seeking nectar from the pink blossoms of a crab apple tree. A small, male indigo bunting flew into an oak tree and began singing its beautiful lyrical song. I smiled at the bird and whispered, "Thank you." A male red cardinal flew overhead towards the bird feeder. He seemed to be in a hurry to feed. He was joined by a female cardinal and a gold finch.

The sun had just risen over the hillside lighting the tops of trees and shrubs. White puffy cumulus clouds began to fill the azure blue sky. A dark emerald green frog, sitting on the edge of the pond, began adding his voice to the chorus of songs. What a perfect day to be in the garden. I took a deep breath and began to slowly relax. A cyan blue dragon fly flew over the pond and landed near a rock that was sitting on the edge of the waterfall. I watched the dragon fly for a long time until my eyes became blurry.

Suddenly, I heard a quiet voice, "Why are you staring at me?" I looked around to see who was talking to me. There was no one. Did I imagine hearing a voice?

"I'm the dragon fly," the voice again spoke to me. I looked down at the dragon fly and said out loud, "I must be dreaming; did I hear you speak?"

"Yes, I'm talking to you, in your mind."

"That's impossible."

"No, it isn't. I'm conveying my thoughts to you and your mind is translating it into your language."

"That's amazing, but why me?"

"You are the caretaker of this garden. You provide food and water for all the creatures, large and small. You place native plants in the garden which are needed for all of us to live. And, you don't use poison on the creatures that eat the plant leaves. All of us are thankful to you for creating this garden and caring for native plants in other gardens in the region. You share your love with us."

I smiled at the dragon fly. Suddenly, he disappeared, and a shimmering blue lapis lazuli blue creature about four inches tall appeared before my eyes. I rubbed my eyes to see if I was dreaming. When I realized that I was awake, I spoke.

"Who are you?"

"I'm a nature spirit."

"Are you like one of the water nymphs in Wagner's operas, *The Ring Cycle*?"

"No, I'm a water spirit, associated with one of the four elements: water, earth, air, and fire. Because you have created a pond and waterfall and planted native plants, we nature spirits are attracted to your garden. We work with you to nourish the seedlings and help them to mature."

"How many nature spirits are here in this garden?"

"There are many of us. We live with the plants. What a joyful experience it is for us when a seed is planted. During this moment, a note of joy is sounded on the etheric plane to listen and come watch as you tend your plants and release positive energy into the soil. When a seed becomes a seedling, for us it's like humans seeing a baby born. Spring time in the garden is a joyful place. For now, I must leave. A larger nature spirit wants to give you a message.

The small blue nature spirit disappeared, and a tall smoky figure appeared hovering over the garden.

"Greetings, I am the guardian of the garden. I watch over the nature spirits and guide them in their work. Together, you and I and the nature spirits have an important duty to the garden's ecosystem, to the region, and to Mother Earth. All creatures depend upon us to nurture and care for gardens and the land."

"You say that you are a guardian of the garden; do you belong to the fairy kingdom?"

"We are called by many names. We are creatures, not humans, living on a subtle energy level. We manifest ourselves in a variety of forms. There are tiny beings or fairies that sleep in the buds of flowers, to garden caretakers, and at the highest level, the archangels. The small creatures are called elves, fairies, goblins, sylphs, and undines. In the ancient language of Sanskrit, there is one word which covers all these beings, *Deva,* which means shining one or being of luminous light. Devas exist in a dimension normally not perceivable by the usual five human senses and incapable of being proven by contemporary science. The devic natural hierarchy is similar to the natural hierarchy of atomic life which also begins in dense matter as in the mineral realm, and which progresses to plant, animal and human. One flow of the devic natural hierarchy could be said to be elemental to elves, to cherubim, to angels, to archangels."

"Thank you for sharing this information."

"Over the past years we have been saddened by all the pollution and destruction of nature's habitats within the environment. More houses and businesses are being built in what were once prairies, fields or glades. Native plants and creatures are losing their habitats, their homes. The bees, butterflies, birds and insects are slowly dying because of this destruction. Also, highway departments are spraying the land along the roads with harmful chemicals destroying native grasses, plants and trees. Global warming is here, primarily because of the greenhouse effect from the burning of fossil fuels."

"I agree; global warming is here and many changes are occurring which are harmful to the ecosystem. However, there are more people today who are concerned and want to help to clean the environment and plant habitats for all creatures."

"We are pleased, but we are concerned that all your efforts may not be enough. We need the whole world's population to change their attitudes and be concerned about caring for nature's creatures and plants. Too many people do not care. They have big grassy lawns that are dead spaces for the habitats of nature's creatures. We appreciate that you, like other people who understand the need, are doing something different in gardens. Many of you have taken the gardening role that transcends the needs of the individual gardener. You understand biodiversity and balance of the ecosystem. You have started planting native plants and trees and removing alien species. And you are working with public and private gardens, introducing native plants and only using a few cultivars."

"We are trying."

"When you are in the garden, have an awareness of us; maintain an open mind and loving attitude. Realize that we want to co-create together, to provide an ecological balance in the garden, the region, and the world. I am pleased that you are now aware of us. We shall meet at another time. Good-by."

I sat there, stunned and in awe of the experience. I realized I had a spiritual experience with a spiritual being. I slowly left the garden and for the next few weeks I began to do a computer search on devic energy and beings. To my surprise I found many books and articles on the subject.

One of the first books that I read was about the Findhorn Garden. In the late 1960s the Findhorn Garden was established. The garden is a spiritual community of gardeners in northern Scotland. Today, it is considered an Ecovillage. The founders and community members describe how over several years they have been in contact with various nature spirits whose messages have helped to produce almost miraculous results with vegetables, fruits, and flowers. One of the messages was: In our world, which is closer to the world of causes, we see that all things are a manifestation of intelligence and that all happenings are related. Human thoughts and states of mind affect the garden. Radiate love in the garden while tending to the plants. The love is the ability to be truly sensitive to the needs, both material and spiritual of the plants in the garden.

In contact with a Landscape Angel in 1969, the message was: We come when there is a call from any part of life. But initiative must come from your side. We do not force ourselves on you. We rejoice at man's cooperation but the rejoicing is because he is reaching out to us. We have always been part of life on Earth and of man's endeavors, but man has been generally unaware of our part. Now his consciousness is broadening to truth, and of course we rejoice.

One of the founders of Findhorn, Dorothy McLean wrote that her contact with the devas opened up in a natural way, rising organically from her life background. She and two brothers were brought up by loving parents in a beautiful old house next to woods in Canada. They had gardens of vegetables and flowers, but she was not especially attracted to cultivated plants. She loved wandering in the wild places. She mediated daily and received messages from an inner guidance. When she worked at the same hotel in Scotland as the original gardeners at Findhorn, she was asked to join them in creating a garden.

One of her first messages from a garden angel was: You are to cooperate in the garden. Begin this by thinking about the nature spirits, the higher over lighting nature spirits, and tune into them. They will be overjoyed to find some members of the human race eager for their help. This is the first step. By the higher nature spirits, I mean those such as the spirits of clouds, of rain and of vegetables. Seek into the glorious realms of nature with sympathy and understanding. Knowing that these beings are of the Light, willing to help, but suspicious of humans and on the lookout for the false, the snags. Keep with Me and they will find none, and you will all build towards the new.

Later, Dorothy wrote a book about her experiences, *To Hear the Angels Sing*. During additional research I came across a book, *Fairies at Work and Play* observed by Geoffrey Hodson in the 1920s while living in England. The book was re-published in 1982 by Quest Books, Theosophical Publishing Company. After many years of meditation Geoffrey Hodson began seeing fairies and other spiritual creatures in his consciousness. He writes in September, 1921 of his experiences seeing fairies in a glade a few miles from his home. He describes the glade as having beautiful old trees, touched with autumn tints, a stream gently flowing and the whole bathed in autumn sunshine. The surface of this field is densely populated by fairies, brownies, elves and a species of grass creature, something between an elf and a brownie, but smaller, and apparently less evolved than either. The fairies are flitting through the air in short flights taking very graceful poses as they fly. They express in the highest degree the qualities of light-heartedness, gaiety and *joie de vivre.* They appear as females, dressed in a white, or very pale pink, clinging, sheeny material of exceedingly fine texture. The limbs are uncovered; the wings are oval, small and elongated.

While visiting the Lake District in November, 1921 he was impressed by the fact that the whole of this district was densely populated with deva life at all levels. He describes the word "deva" as a host of "shining ones" of almost infinite variety of form and function. There are tiny nature-spirit, brownie, manikin, gnome, and fairy, up to the individualized orders of nature-devas. Broadly speaking, the lower types remain near the surface of the earth; there is a clan of fairies apparently approaching individualization and possessing both intelligence and will-power, which rises to considerable heights; the upper air and mountain summits are occupied by the various nature-devas; it would appear that these last rarely descend to the bottom of the valley, and much more frequently rise to great heights in the air.

Dr. Rudolf Stiner, in his article in 1923, *Plant World and the Elemental Nature Spirit* wrote that fairies are spirit, embodied in the idea of Mother Nature. They are connected to the four elements, earth, air, fire, and water.

I have met several people in my life who have claimed to have seen and communicated with these fairies, devas and elementals using their third eye or enhanced sensory perception. Dora van Gelder wrote *The Real World of Fairies, A Personal Account.* She is also a co-founder of the *Healing Touch*, a healing method of laying on hands by nurses with their patients.

While living in Illinois, a few years ago, I had an appointment with a healer to check to see if I had any health or psychic problems. After the session was over, she said, "Are you aware that you have nature spirits hovering around you?"

"No," I said, "I was unaware." I was shocked; could it be true?

She also said that what she perceived reminded her of the fairy painting by Edward Robert Hughes, "Midsummer Eve," a 1908 Victorian painting.

How did she do that? Or, was that her imagination? Could I trust her perception?" After the session I looked up the painting on the web. The painting was of little nature spirits circling the feet of a young woman. Did I look like that to the healer? I was surprised.

I shared my experiences with my sister and brother-in-law. Both of them have had experiences with nature creatures. They were not surprised with my story about meeting a deva. Many years ago my brother-in-law wrote an article describing his experience. He gave me the article to read:

One day I was in Texas, a land of wide open spaces with scattered trees growing along the waterways or bayous. In a quiet meditative space that I had created, I began to observe and become aware of the deva evolution. Beings of the devidic evolution are all around us. Their energy makes up our bodies, creates the greenery, nourishes all living things, be they mineral, vegetable, animal, or man. Although it may be difficult to think that we share our world with other evolutionary entities, yet it is true. There has been throughout recorded history, attempts to understand, manipulate and appreciate this evolutionary wave.

If you have ever sat in the park, gone to the river or ocean, climbed a hill or mountain height, felt peace and serenity or power of the outdoors, then you were feeling the results of the energy of the entities which make up this all-inclusive alternate evolution.

In reality, devas are not much concerned with humankind; they have their own tasks to accomplish. There are a few orders among them which concern themselves with humanity, nevertheless the vast majority of devas follow their path until they becomes the most crystallized forms on the physical/etheric plane.

Whether you believe or not believe in fairies or devas, it is important to following their directives. We must learn to transcend our personal needs for beauty of cultivated plants from other countries and large grass lawns, that don't attract pollinators, and become aware of the environment, the ecosystem that we live in. Global warming is a threat to the planet. Bees, butterflies and birds are dying.

Dr. Doug Tallamy, a professor at the University of Delaware has written: "As gardeners and stewards of our land, we have never been so empowered to help save biodiversity from extinction, and the need to do so has never been so great. All we need to do is plant native plants."

Mariellen Griffith is an artist, photographer, and writer living near Eureka Springs, Arkansas. She is a member of the Garden Writer's Association, the National Wildlife Association, The National Audubon Society, The Eureka Springs Historical Society, life member of the Carroll County, Arkansas Master Gardeners, life member of the Arkansas Native Plant Society, and Certified Member of the Northwest Arkansas Master Naturalist. She is Professor Emeritus, Butler University in Indianapolis, Indiana, where she taught for twenty-six years.

16-Aadya's Long Walk

By

Ruth Mitchell

A wedding scene between Aadya and Poma from *The Two Moons of Merth*, a fantasy saga of the royal Karda family.

* * *

Entering the hallway, Aadya can hear the music reverberating throughout the expanse of Katara. There are stringed instruments and drums and a magnificent machine that creates musical vibrations with pipes and clashing metal discs. When the guards open the gargantuan doors to the Cathedral, she is shocked to see how many people are present and waiting for the ceremony to begin. A blast from musical horns above her startles her so much she almost drops her bouquet that cascades from her waist to the floor. The heady fragrance of the flowers, now enhanced by the elixir she was given, swirls up around her with its own mesmerizing spell.

It feels like the only thing keeping her from floating off up into the rafters of the Great Hall is the magnificent gown that lies across her chest. Her small bronze shoulders are bare, and at her throat, encrusted with shimmering jewels, is the symbolic chamra, the same spellcaster Queen Mesa wore on her wedding day. The tingling sensation from the strange elixir still flows through her veins and she feels fearless. As if to remind her, she is protected, her breath is sometimes visible in traces of swirly vapor, but mostly she feels as if she is outside her body; she herself is a spectator in this grand parade.

Her first glimpse of Poma sets her heart to pounding so hard she gulps in air. He is waiting for her at the end of the aisle, with his brothers at his side. His gaze is firmly focused on the vision of her in the astonishing gown. I want this feeling to last forever!

And the walk, as tedious and filled with drama as it is, feels like an infinite passage as each step she takes is a deliberate passage of time. So, that when she arrives at Poma's side, she has evolved. She has metamorphosed into something greater than she was at the beginning of her journey down the long hall.

He extends his arm to her and when she touches him, feels a new sensation, a warm tingling bolt that travels up her arm and then gently strikes into her heart. It is as if he feels it too and he leans in to steady her. "My heart is filled with love, you are such an incredible creature," he whispers.

She wants to respond but it is as if her vocal cords have been frozen and so she nods to him, with a slight and respectful bow of her head. In what plausible world am I an incredible creature? I belong in the woods with my fearless and muddy dogs.

Later she would not be able to recall the words they spoke, only that a white silk scarf had been symbolically tied around their wrists. Once she and the dress, with its long train, are turned, she and Poma walk triumphantly down the aisle as cheers by the crowd resonate across the chasm of the enormous room. Waiting attendants escort them to the Matong chamber where they are met by the King and Queen.

The four of them are glowing with the emotion the bridal vows have imprinted on their minds, but not a word is said. They have rehearsed this part, so Aadya knows just what to do though the volume of the dress with its long train sends a sudden burst of panic through her body. The gossamer attendants appear from nowhere and lift up the length of the gown and fold it delicately to accommodate the small chamber. She kneels on a stool placed before her and faces the prince who kisses her hand and beckons her to rise. This is symbolic of her respect and humility for the powers of the Matong.

The bride and groom then face King Larsa and Queen Mesa together who return their motions of bows and lowered heads, gestures of humility and respect. Poma leads Aadya over to the shimmering Matong and places her hands onto the glowing orb. She is met with a surge of energy filling her with a thousand thoughts rushing into her mind like a stream bursting from the obstruction of a jammed log in an early spring snow melt. Her mind, already influenced by the contents she consumed from the golden chalice earlier in the day, is afire with sensations. She hears herself say, "I will." But she is not certain to what or to whom she is saying this. Feeling strangely depleted and renewed at the same time, she looks weakly toward Poma for guidance who looks absolutely tantalizing to her, as he begins to stream his thoughts into her mind.

SOON WE WILL BE TOGETHER. WE WILL TOUCH AND BECOME ONE AND THE ECTASY WILL BE ALL.

YES. I AM YOURS. It is the first time she is aware of her thoughts being projected to Poma. And also, the first time it doesn't alarm her when he responds inside her head.

Poma bends over with his steel grey eyes focused on hers and kisses Aadya's hand. WE ARE ENCOURAGED TO BE ALONE NOW BEFORE THE GREAT FEAST. IT SHOWS WE ARE HUNGRY FOR EACH OTHER. OUR CHAMBERS HAVE BEEN PREPARED FOR US.

Aadya lets a drowsy giggle escape from her pursed lips. LET US GO THEN. All apprehension about being with him is gone. I can't wait!

Ruth Mitchell's career as a travel writer took her many places. Her gigs as a freelancer educated her in the ways of the world. Ruth is the author of three very diverse books.

(https://emerge-writerscolony.org/author/ruth-mitchell/)

Childhood

By

Fred Yu

Last night, I dreamed that I died. The dull pain, residual agony that even morphine could not uproot, ebbed away with a hollow heaving of the chest.

First, there was silence. The endless beeping from the hospital equipment faded, and I thought I heard my children breathe a sigh of relief. Then, I heard weeping. It was my aging wife, failing to recognize that suffering finally came to an end. And somewhere in the background, in a whisper, I thought I heard my son say, "Goodbye Dad. Take care of yourself out there…"

In the distance, somewhere in the vast open space, I heard the familiar sounds of celebration. I couldn't open my eyes. I didn't know where I was. They say that some people went to heaven in all its brightness and glory. Some people go to hell, where groping flames scorched the flesh and every sound repeated itself in cold echoes. When I finally opened my eyes, I saw my parents.

They looked much younger, like how I remembered them when I was a child, when they were in their prime. They hovered over me, peered into my face with a strange curiosity, almost afraid that I would recognize them. There was a glow of pride in my Dad's face. Last time I saw him like that was when I told him I was accepted to Princeton.

I stared into a well-lit room both warm and cozy with all the material comfort I've come to expect. The white cotton surface under me was soft, very much like my own bed. I was still in a lot of pain, though nothing like the days before I died. Maybe that extra shot of morphine followed me into the afterlife.

I tried to turn my body but a sharp pain flashed through my chest. I winced.

A warm hand brushed across my forehead. "Take it easy," my mother said. "You'll be feeling better in no time."

Another man, someone I didn't recognize, was speaking to my dad in the background. "The cancer will go away in a few months," he said, with authority. "Everything else is normal. He came with bad eyesight. That'll be a few months. Bad hips and knees, trouble urinating, arthritis in the fingers. All the basic stuff. Should go away in time. Looks like he'll have a great start in death."

My dad breathed a sigh of relief. My mother was giggling. "See?" she said to me. "Nothing to worry about."

"Where am I?"

My dad hovered over me. "You're in a new world. This'll be home for a long time."

"New world," my mother repeated. "Of course, you're still in the same place. Just that you can't see them, and they can't see you."

I closed my eyes. The pain was unbearable. "Who's

them?"

"Them? All the people you left behind."

"Where's my wife?"

"No rush. Eventually, she'll come."

"It's still early," my dad said. "We're going to a party tonight. Your party. Everyone's going to show up."

My head was still spinning and the pain was not retreating. I could hardly remember what was said to me. At some point, when fatigue and suffering washed away all cognitive thinking, it no longer mattered whether I was alive or dead, in hell or in paradise. I just wanted to close my eyes and fade away.

I didn't know how long I was asleep, but I opened my eyes to my father's calm voice. "Wake up, sleepy head. It's party time."

The room was much darker then, with a single light from somewhere in the room casting soft shadows on a barren wheelchair next to me. My father was dressing it. Layer upon layer of heavy blankets were lined along the seat and the back rest.

"It's cold outside. We can just walk there. Your mother is already there."

He lifted me into the wheelchair, covered me with more blankets, and pushed me out of my room.

My head was still spinning. The air was suddenly cold and raw. I could barely open my eyes, and the few instances when I managed to look around, I noticed that the world was a blur, as if engulfed in thick fog and mist. There were lights everywhere, like in any other town, and the sounds of voices and footsteps were ample. I felt better, tried to look around but my eyes were heavy and my thoughts were scattered. I thought I fell asleep again.

A loud voice brought me to my senses. "You're here! You're here!"

A huge man was sprinting at me with arms outstretched. I recognized the voice.

"They told me you're finally here!" the large man shouted, engulfing me in a tight embrace.

"Easy John," my father said. "He's still hurting."

John released me. "So what? He'll stop hurting in no time." He looked at me with a big smile. "So good to see you. So good to see you again."

My cousin John looked much younger than when he died in a car accident twenty years ago. His face, his build, his body language reminded me of our younger days cliff diving together in Jamaica, when he needed three shots of over-proof rum before coming up with the guts to ask a girl to dance. And here he was, in front of me, myself an old and crippled man while he looked as fit and vibrant as ever.

"I hardly recognize you, John," I said. John ran behind me and grabbed the handles to the wheelchair. "Let's go. Everyone's waiting. Dave made two hundred candles for this party, and his wife lit them all just now. The place is glowing bright."

"Dave?"

"Come on, you remember Dave. His wife came over last year."

I sat up. "Really?"

"She had a heart attack or something," my father said.

"Surprised it took her so long. She wanted to come here ever since Dave came."

I didn't say anything then. Dave and his wife went to high school together, and were lovebirds from day one. I used to see them smooching in the back of the school building. I was there when he said his wedding vows, when he said, "Till death do us part."

"Yeah, a bad heart attack," John said, pushing my wheelchair faster now. "She was clutching her chest for the longest time. The pain took forever to go away."

"You know who else is going to be there?" my father asked with a chuckle.

"Grandpa," I said.

He paused. "Yeah, he'll be there too."

All of a sudden, we emerged into the banquet room. It was crowded but bright, noisy but organized. All two hundred candles were illuminated, as expected, and the massive room was glowing with energy. The guests have all arrived, and they were waiting.

Then, a long drawn out round of applause, as if I've achieved something substantial in my first night of death. I looked into each of the guests, and for a moment, horrified at how many I recognized. Except they were different. Every one of them seemed younger and healthier than what I remembered.

My brother Ray came up to help me out of my wheelchair. He had a stroke a few years ago and was found dead in the bathroom. I will never forget. I cried through his funeral, and said nothing to his daughter, his wife, for weeks. I just didn't know what to say. And now, he appeared before me, both limber and agile. I could hardly believe my eyes.

Ray lifted me, a vibrant smile on his face, and settled me in a seat at the head table. "Welcome," he said with a laugh. "Surprised? Never thought you'd see me here, huh?"

"What's going on, Ray? What's happening here?"

"Nothing much," Ray said, laughing again. "We're celebrating. For you."

The guests gathered around me, some with wine in their hands, others simply stepped up to pat me on the back. All around me were familiar faces, happy faces, each truly glad to see me in the afterlife. Cousins, uncles, friends, a niece who died last year, old binge drinking buddies from college, all hovered over me as if I was a superstar.

Eventually, everyone returned to their seats and appetizers were served. A group of children were running around the tables, laughing and tossing a rubber ball between them. The adults ignored them, mostly, except for a few harsh words here and there, released in a routine manner. The kids were loud and disruptive, but I felt good watching the children at play.

Ray sat next to me and placed a hand on my shoulder. "Don't worry," he said. "You'll get used to everything here. Everyone does. You can always ask me if you need to know anything."

My head was spinning. I had so many questions, but I couldn't remember any of them. Everyone was chatting and eating and drinking, drowned in the laughter of so many; and yet, all I could do was stare blankly at the festivities. Entrees were served. Everything resembled the world that I was used to, as if life, or death, had never changed.

"What're you gonna do here?" I thought I heard someone ask.

"He'll probably be a doctor again," my father responded.

"That's great! Not enough doctors in this world."

A little boy ran up to me with a smile on his face. He was holding a rubber ball and he wanted to throw it at me.

"Go play somewhere else," Ray said.

I reached out and tickled the boy's chubby cheeks.

"Hey, what's your name?"

"Bob."

"Hey Bob," I said, stroking his forehead. "Is that your ball?"

"Yes."

"Yeah? And, what are you doing here, little boy?"

"I'm here for my grandson's party."

"Okay." Ray stood up from his seat and reached over.

"Go play somewhere else."

Bob backed away. He stuck out his tongue, then turned and ran.

I leaned back into my chair and waited for Ray to sit down again. He seemed uneasy. "Cute kid," I said, reaching for my glass of wine. "So who's his grandson?"

"You are."

I froze. "What... what did you just say?"

"Listen to me," Ray said, holding up both his palms as if to stop me from jumping on him. "Listen to me. You'll get used to this world soon enough."

"Grandpa died an old man. He was a successful, respected man."

"And he came here as an old man," Ray said with a sigh. "And you did too."

A hand fell on my shoulder behind me. It was John. "I'm sorry you came so late. Grandpa took a turn for the worse just this year. He's close to the end of his death."

Ray took a deep breath. "I didn't want to explain it to you yet because you just got here. All the little ones you see running around. We're all going to end up like that. As you go on in death, you become younger and physically stronger. But some years before the end, like these kids, everyone loses their mind. Everyone loses their ability to reason, to speak. Ultimately, everyone loses the ability to feed themselves and use the toilet. That's what happens at the end of death. For everyone. We become vegetables. We can't communicate. We can only cry."

There was silence. John patted my shoulder again, speechless. I stared at the children running around the banquet hall, giggling and tossing the ball at each other.

"See how they're giggling like little imbeciles?" John finally said. "It's almost the end for them. Grandpa's attention span was the first to go. When he became much too naïve, we asked him to retire. That wasn't so long ago."

"And what happens next?" I asked. I pointed and swallowed hard. "To them."

"They'll lose their ability to talk, and they won't be able to walk anymore," Ray responded. "They'll make a mess everywhere so they'll have to wear diapers until the end of their deaths. Some progress faster than others. Grandpa will have to go to a daycare center so we can work during the day."

"And then?"

"And then they go. And some people say that they'll be born somewhere and they'll start life."

John pulled up a chair and sat down next to me. "Some people have shorter deaths, and no one really knows why. But as time goes on, everyone's mind deteriorates." He points to the children in the distance. "They're losing their grip on their emotions. Instant gratification is a disease. It gets out of control. By adolescence, each one forgets his knowledge and experience. They pursue small, insignificant goals. It's heartbreaking."

For a long time, no one could say anything, each thinking his own thoughts, his own worries. Finally, John said, "Everyone's afraid of suddenly reincarnating. I guess no one wants to lose their current memories. We're going to reincarnate into an unknown land, you know. Not that anyone knows for sure we'll be reincarnated. But I enjoyed my life, and I'm enjoying my death. Really no big deal to be born somewhere. I'll look forward to some hot chick waiting for me in my high school science class again." He laughed. I squeezed my eyes shut. "I just..." John's voice broke. "I just don't want to be like them for too long. You know, Grandpa was really something. But look at him now. To think that he cried because he dropped his ice-cream bar. One day he won't even know how to use the toilet..."

I opened my eyes. John was close to tears. "I just don't want that," the big man said. "I just don't want..."

My father walked over, the smile on his face quickly fading when he saw the frown between my brows. "How're we doing?" he asked.

No one answered. He tapped Ray on the shoulder and motioned for him to go away. Ray nodded and picked himself up. Dad sat down, reached for the wine and filled my glass. "How're we doing?" he asked again.

"Doing great," I responded. "Just learning new things, you know, about this world."

"That's great," he said. "It's important to learn as much as you can in the beginning. As time goes on, you'll get used to things here and everything will be fine."

Dessert was placed before me. Some of the guests were already approaching my table to say good night, but a few recognized the tension on my face and simply waved from a distance. I tried to smile back, but couldn't. Perhaps everyone here was already used to the confusion of the newcomers.

"Dad, I wasn't born yesterday," I said. "You know why you sat down and asked Ray to go away."

He was silent, staring at me, as if to look deep into my soul, and vague memories of how he used to do that emerged. His habits haven't changed, after all.

"You'll do just fine," he finally said. "We'll teach you everything you need to know, and you'll do just fine in this world."

"This world," I said, my voice rising. "This world is what?"

"Do you want the scoop on economics and supply and demand here?" he asked in a commanding tone. "You just arrived. You should be enjoying yourself."

"Enjoy what?"

"Your pain will be gone soon. You can enjoy anything you want."

"How?" My voice was raised, and I regretted the moment I saw the look in his eyes. I remembered that look.

"I don't see what you're unhappy about. You just got here. Time is on your side. Everything is ahead of you. You have more time than anyone else here."

"More time for what?"

"For anything you want! You have the chance to do whatever you want with yourself. Maybe you'll do something great here!"

"Maybe," I repeated.

"Yes, maybe," my dad said, his voice now a whisper. "Stop worrying about it so soon. It's only childhood. Everyone goes through it."

Slowly, the banquet hall was emptied. The guests stopped by to shake hands with my mother and with Ray. No one came to interrupt.

There was a burst of screams. I jerked back to look. Grandpa was on his belly, pounding the floor with his fists in a tantrum. He was right under the doorframe of the banquet hall, and the last few guests trying to leave the premises were stepping around him to get through the door. They tried to avoid looking at him, and hurried away as soon as they passed.

"I don't want to leave! I don't want to leave!" he was shouting.

John was hovering over him. "Let's go, Grandpa."

"I'm not leaving!" Grandpa was crying hard. He rolled over and tried to kick John in the shin.

"Okay, then stay." The big man turned to go.

"I'm not staying! I'm not staying!"

John spun around. "Then get up and let's go!"

"I don't want to leave! I don't want to leave!" Grandpa screamed in long, wailing sobs. John shook his head, threw a glance at me from the distance and turned around again. Not far from the door, another kid was throwing a tantrum. I couldn't quite make out what he needed.

A warm hand fell on my shoulder. "Dad?" I asked. "Is this what's in our future?"

"Sooner for me than for you."

John was peeling my grandfather off the floor and strapping him into a stroller. Grandpa continued to kick and scream. John squeezed the buckles, ignored the protests, and pushed the boy away. His screams echoed in the banquet hall.

For the longest time, I thought I still heard Grandpa's screams. Then, suddenly, the room was completely quiet. The other kid was already gone.

"Are you happy for your grandpa?" my father asked, out of nowhere.

My lips quivered, but I couldn't speak.

"Why not?" he asked with a sigh.

I lowered my head.

"You know how happy I was, pushing your wheelchair

into this party? I don't know if the days ahead are going to be good for you. I don't know if your time in the afterlife is going to be glorious."

I didn't say anything, didn't look at him.

He continued. "John was pushing your grandpa in the stroller, almost the same way. Your grandpa already had a great time here. He accomplished a lot. Everyone knows it. But is anyone happy for him? Everyone is happy for you, enough for a celebration. And no one knows whether you'll have decent years ahead of you."

My father lifted the glass of wine and gulped it down in one breath. "Just because time moves forward, and you're at the beginning and your grandpa is at the end. Your grandpa did great. John should be happier pushing that stroller."

The banquet hall was completely silent then, except for the sound of breathing, my breathing. The night flew by, or did it? It may be morning soon, though I have yet to see a morning in the afterlife. But I looked forward to it. The birds may chirp outside, the early smell of wet air would fill my lungs and little squirrels would be prancing around the lawn. But then, maybe there's no such thing. If I waited long enough in this silence, the sun would shine through the massive windows on both sides of the room, and silver light would flood every tile and fabric in the banquet hall. At least that's what I hoped would happen next.

Just yesterday, I was afraid of the end of my life. Today I'm afraid of the end of my death. Why do I always fear tomorrow?

107

I Am Not

By

Fred Yu

I should have been a snare for human connections,
Licensed to coddle egos at risk,
Swimming in words of praise each day,
Drowning in loneliness with each encounter,
But I am not that man.

I could have been the stranger who screamed injustice
To urge those offended to speak,
Riding the glory of a man outraged,
Clawing through the web of blame each day,
But I am not that person.

I would have been the leader who called for action,
Enticed to stand for something,
Bloated from triumph of wish fulfilled,
Enslaved by an ideal I cannot abandon,
But I am a different person.

I wasn't the hero who sacrificed integrity and honor,
Nor the hustler who wrote poems about etiquette,
I've forsaken the praise for a glass of wine,
Exchanged the glory for a moment of silence,

Abandoned the triumph for vague simplicity,
To avoid pondering the face of that person.

Fred Yu writes fiction in the Asian Historical Fantasy genre. He is a filmmaker, chef, Feng Shui practitioner, martial artist, and for over a decade was a risk manager in a global bank. He graduated from New York University majoring in film and television.

Yu's publications in the Historical Asian Fantasy genre include, *The Legend of Snow Wolf* and *The Orchid Farmer's Sacrifice*. He has also published a cookbook, *Haute Tea Cuisine*, as well as a martial arts instructional book, *Yin Yang Blades*.

Yu is currently a full-time writer and lives in New York City.

(https://fredyuauthor.com/)

My dealings with the book, POEMCRAZY by Susan G. Wooldridge, Three Rivers Press, 1996.

By

Pat Laster

As my close associates know, I try to annotate where I found or bought a book, and then to note the time and date I began and ended each reading session. One of my husbands (may he rest in peace) asked me once why I did that. I don't remember my answer; I only remember his asking.

This 210-page paperback book has been mine since I found it at Raney's Flea Market in Mayflower, AR, on December 13, 2008. After monthly sessions of the now-defunct group, Central Arkansas Writers, which met in a room at the Faulkner County library in Conway, I always liked to pull off the freeway into the edge of the small, river-front community. So I've had this book for thirteen years.

The first notes I made were on December 16 that year, and included boxes around unusual surnames, a section of my then-in-progress *Compendium of Journal Jottings*. These names were in the Acknowledgments page: Chalk, Fay, Shanks, BigEagle, Centolella and Grapes.

A Digression--Pablo Neruda:
Rereading this book in 2021, my first marking was

111

boxing in the epigraph: ". . . Poetry arrived/ in search of me. I don't know, I don't know where/ it came from, from winter or a river./ I don't know how or when . . ..—Pablo Neruda." My notes—in ink: "Use this as a take-off on the beginnings of my writing." Neruda is especially dear to me—I have his *Book of Questions*—and even drafted a poem based on one of his questions:

Gloves or bare hands?
And when you change the landscape
is it with bare hands or with gloves?
~Pablo Neruda, **The Book of Questions**

and during an MFA workshop, we read his "Ode to a Large Tuna in the Market." I wanted to find this book, so I went to my poetry book shelves. With no flashlight and kneeling on the loveseat directly in front of the shelf, I looked down the top shelf from right to left. At the very end, I saw an inch-thick book with Neruda's name on it. Wha. . .? I pulled it down. *Residence on Earth* Bilingual Introduction by Jim Harrison. Opening it, I found an answer: "7/16 Sisters' trip, Crossville TN 50 cents." I didn't remember. But I brought it to my reading area. Why not read this one, too? Pretend you're still in an MFA workshop. So, on September 4, 2021, at 11:10 p.m. I began. Most days, I'd read an hour in the afternoon and an hour at night. I finished it on September 13 at 1:35 p.m. Trying to find a translated-from-Spanish connection to what I know as present-day poetry, I penciled circles around his many, many likes and a little alliteration. I also marked a poem I thought suitable as a funeral reading.

But goodness! How I've digressed. Now back to *Poemcrazy.*

Another Diversion-- e. e. cummings:

It was July 4 of 2021, a Sunday at 11:09 pm when I next opened this book. Why now, I wonder? It could be that I had decided I needed to increase my income from writing to match the expenses. I had already entered Arizona's State Poetry contest shortly after it opened in June. The Arkansas, Missouri and Tennessee societies also had upcoming contests. I needed inspiration. For whatever reason, after reading a bit of the Iliad, like an entrée of hated liver-and-onions, I needed something different to cleanse my palate. Here is my note on page eight in the Wooldridge book written on the same night: "Why am I reading a child's version of the Iliad? Because I thought I needed to know the story. But it's so grisly—even the Scholastic version." Even with its colorful illustrations.

In the chapter—all chapters were short; some with exercises at the end—"collecting words/creating a word pool," she listed hum, fizz, fiddle, fandango and several more. I added "voila, enigma, eschew, preclude and detritus. But I didn't do the exercise.

Two nights later, I underlined this: "[e .e.] cummings reminds me to allow poems to swagger, soar or tiptoe in unexpectedly. . . Poems aren't written from ideas...and they're not overly controlled." Hmm. "Read some poems by e. e. cummings," she suggested. I do have a cummings

113

book in my poetry shelf, and I've reformed a poem into a look-alike cummings poem. The content of the poem is not necessarily like cummings, but the formatting is.

April showers
—under the influence of e. e. cummings

Ap
ril gobb
(led)
up
Mar
Chwinds--R
eser(ved)
them untIl all
gull(
ible)eager plan
/tl overs tru
ndled them out
Sureen
oughAprilH
itOurparto
fourW
orldwithw
ind&show
ersEver
yday un
tilallmo
isturew(as
wRung)fr

omtheclou
dsleav
ingus
Soa
ked--(bu
t)happy.

The poet who judged the April monthly told me later, after I admitted which poem I entered, "Oh, when I saw that, I put it aside; I wasn't judging that!" This poem drove spell-check into red-lined vapors.

More Poetic--Ideas:

Wooldridge quotes myriad poets: Gary Snyder, Richard Wilbur, Joy Harjo (current National Poet Laureate), A. A. Milne, Stanley Kunitz, Allen Ginsburg, Walt Whitman, and many more well-known names. I own books from many of them. In the chapter *full moon me* I underlined these sentences: "Writing about ourselves doesn't mean we're self-involved. We have to start with ourselves before we can reach beyond ourselves. . . . the way we see and write about the world always reveals who we are."

Thinking About One's Grandmothers:

Chapter 18, *from my grandmother,* is circled and my note under it reads: "Which am I more like, Grandmother (paternal) or Grandma (maternal)?" Wooldridge suggests later that readers may "want to focus on one family member who helped form you." And my answer: "Who would that be, Grandma Flossie or Grandmother Mabel?"

So I began writing to figure it out, as if it makes any difference this far out.

Grandmother Mabel Horton Couch
a Mesostich acrostic

 Grandmother (paternal) Mabel **r**efused to leave her new home **a**nd her children
to move to Houston with **N**oah, her husband. She **d**etermined to stay in Arkansas.
They divorced. He **m**arried again. She never did. **O**ne of my sibs remembers her
still living in **t**his house, to which we moved in 1942. **H**owever, Hubert, her only
son and our dad, **e**ventually bought land across our gravel **r**oad, built her a small
home.

My remembrances: she dipped snuff, quilted, **a**nd had a canary. Burying an old
iron pot, Dad **b**uilt her a fishpond. She'd sit out **e**venings before dark. At her
death, I **l**atched on to her oak secretary (I still

Have it) and her footed, flared drinking glasses **o**rnamented around the tops
with colored lines. **R**arely was she seen without a brooch on the bosom of
her long dress. **T**hose, and her other jewelry went to her girls and theirs **o**n her

death. Porch boxes of lantana sparked my nascent
love of flowers. I grow
lantanas, too.

Camp meeting time found her 'tenting on the
grounds' until the powers-
that-be tore all tents down. Cabins, some called
them. Though lame, though
alone, her strength and stoicism and
determination inspired me.

Her favorite hymn was "Love, Mercy and Grace," by C.
Austin Miles, page 153 in the Cokesbury Hymnal. Family
lore says that on her deathbed, she moaned, "But who'll
take care of Hubert?"
Grandma Flossie, Mom's mother, seemed more tender,
malleable, and loveable than Grandmother. A widow for
many years, she was kind and considerate. Before
Grandpa Elmer died of peritonitis, they had birthed eight
children. Mom was the second oldest. We lived, as the
crow flies, within a good mile if we walked through the
woods. Once, I took my four children and left my
husband and their daddy. I went to her house. By then,
she'd married Thurman Severn who lived across the creek
and, when Hurricane Lake was built, next to the lake. My
husband, a teacher and journalism sponsor, had gone—
over my protestations that by now he should have enough
sports photos for the paper and the yearbook. He went
anyway. Of course, Grandma shunted me back home, but
I left Art a note: "I left you tonight." I don't know if it did

117

any good thereafter or not. But I never walked out again until the divorce fifteen years later.

Back to *Poemcrazy:*

On page 76, at her chapter, "listening to our shadow," I underlined a paragraph about what Carl Jung said about the first six or so years of our lives, that "when we're about seven, we separate from, then bury or repress, whatever parts of us don't seem to be acceptable in the world around us. According to Jung, these unacceptable parts become our shadow." I thought about adding this to the beginning of my memoir, but I may not. This shadow business is a new concept for me. Is this why I can't or don't remember anything about the house we lived in and the first six years of my life there? Oh, through photos and after years of passing by the "little house" a quarter mile south of where we moved to when I was six, I can remember the outside, rock like this house I grew up in and, two decades ago, moved back into.

Similarly, in her chapter, "coyote and the wild," she stated—and I underlined—"We all have a troublemaker inside ourselves." Another new concept for this octogenarian. She suggests we readers, "Find the nearest place you can with wilderness in it. Drive if you must, even for an hour. . ." I had to laugh. I have wilderness within my acre! I've dedicated the southwest corner of this acre as a "Wendell Berry Preserve," meaning I will not bother the vegetation—vines, crape myrtle, a gum tree, privet bushes—but leave it as is. The birds live there. The corner abuts and encroaches on a neighbor's back yard and I've given him leave—it's his legal right—to trim anything that gets in his way. I've had a tough time keeping to my intention, but there are plenty more places overrun with privet and honeysuckle to try and keep contained. This corner doesn't seem to spread outward, just upward.

In a following chapter, Wooldridge's "practice" suggestions are longer than her discussion of the subject. The final suggestion was "Do anything new." I did. Here's the result:

Do anything new,
she said. New.
Every time, every
thing I write is new.
Oh, the words are old
but the put-togetherness
is always new,
so that every poem,
every word I write
is new in its place.
I wrote something new.

The Center of Your House?

Writing about the center of our houses, Wooldridge says, can take us to the center of ourselves. Since I'm living in the house I grew up in, this sounded easy. So, with my pen and journal in hand, I visited each room, thinking back to childhood and youth. I wrote several pages while recalling early structural changes throughout, the addition later of a bathroom where space was dedicated. But I ended the trip without feeling that one particular room was my "go to" space.

The living room held the old upright piano that I practiced on every day. The sunroom off one side of the living room I didn't use for anything as a youngster, though today, it is my office. The new windows are fronted with shelves of cobalt glass. Bookcases and work tables and filing cabinets and desks provide easy access to anything I need. The dining room leading to and through the rest of the house, besides having a door to the attic, was a pass-through to the kitchen, and later, to the hall, bathroom and three bedrooms. Plus the door to the cellar that was always locked high up. Today, the dining room is my bill-paying office, my meal place, my puzzle-working space, my bird-watching base. Two china cabinets, a buffet matching the oak pedestal table fill out the room's furnishings. It's still a pass through to the rest of the house.

My answer to the center of my house is this: if I'm cooking, it's the kitchen. If I'm eating, reading the paper, working the puzzles, watching the birds, it's the dining room. If I'm reading, it's the living room (I rarely play the Baldwin studio model piano I've had since 1960). If I'm writing, the center of the house is the sunroom-office. And when I'm in one of those places, it's the center of myself.

Do I Have An Image Angel?

The author recalls hearing that in ancient Syrian, "image" meant both icon and angel. Then she writes about images and how and where they appear and how they connect both the physical world and the divine. I'm not much for shadows, ghosts, or angels, though I have felt a guardian-angel touch or two in the past.

But I wrote down an anecdote at the end of this chapter: Image angel (written mid-August of 2021): I found tomatoes left on a white plastic chair on the front porch one Sunday afternoon. Cold tomatoes, not all red, still greenish around the stems. Who was the angel who left these? I was napping and if the angel rang the doorbell, I didn't hear it. I keep the bedroom door closed while I nap to keep the AC's cool air in the room (the AC's off while I sleep).

Turns out, it was a friend and fellow church member, Stanley, who shared his garden produce with me and others at church. He came a second time with more tomatoes, and I sent him home bearing freshly-made pear butter and two halves of a raw pepper stuffed with a cream cheese-celery-ham filling.

Moments of Awareness Leading to a Shift:

Finally, while considering all the shifts in my long life, I was cleaning out the Bermuda grass and horse nettles from the roadside yucca-iris bed. I thought of a present-day shift. New poems often begin with an acrostic, as did this one, shifting from my point of view to . . . well, here it is:

Be careful with that mattock, woman!
Even tho' I'm in your iris bed. It's
Rare, if not impossible, to stop growing
Merely because you laid down a line of rocks. I'll
Undermine them and snake under
Damp rhizomes making it harder to
Attack without uprooting the iris.

Gangs of us work together to make
Radiantly green and lush lawns
And yards. Our instinct is to
Spread—roots underground, stems above when not
mowed.
Sabotage us as you will, but you cannot kill us.
(August 20, 2021, PL)

If You're Looking For Writing Prompts:

Despite its title, *Poemcrazy* will give every reader myriad ideas for all kinds of writing. Her shared experiences are enough to incite memories of your own.
Tell her Pat sent you.

The End

Pat Couch Laster is an Arkansas native. She earned a B.A. from Hendrix College, and a M. Music Ed. from U of A in Fayetteville. She also did graduate work at San Diego State College. After teaching for 27 years, the writing bug bit. She was mentored by Ted O. Badger and

122

the late Robert Speiss. In 2013, she was appointed poetry editor of *Calliope: A Writer's Workshop by Mail.*

A novel and a sequel were followed by a collection of short stories and long poems, *Hiding Myself into Safety.* Her present projects are a memoir, *When I had Another Name* and a poetry collection.

Her website is www.Patlaster.com

A Country Yet to Be

*After the artwork "Untitled (a flag for John Lewis or a
green screen placeholder for an America yet to be") by
Adrian Aguilera/Betelhem Makonnen*

By

Zhenya Yevtushenko

I want to
open a new
country like an old farmhouse
window off-white paint
flaking and creaking
from low distant
thunder.

I want to
sing its anthem
slowly like a lovesong
building and rising until
it drifts in decrescendo
like an autumn leaf
from its mother tree.

I want to
hear it calling
for other fallen leaves
like sisters and brothers
who meet with praying hands
to wish for one thing, and one thing only-
a neverending beginning

I want to
stand under its flag that
looks at me with newborn eyes
which know not to separate the words
mystery-hope-dream-reality
because they still stand
in unity.

I want to
weep for innocence,
for its citizens that
has never known
blood or borders
because one day
they might.

I want to
join them in exalted allegiance
on the ground under
the blanket of those
that came before
and those that
come after.

I want to
reincarnate countries
new and dead to hold
again their hearts
with trembling, calloused hands,
to watch their brittle glory
fade back into the soil,

as they redeem our soul,
fallen but not yet rotted.

Zhenya Yevtushenko is one of the sons of the poet Yevgeny Yevtushenko. When he isn't walking his little dog or struggling with his mental health, Zhenya likes to claim that he is still pursuing his undergraduate degrees in English, Political Science, and History. His works and translations have appeared in *eMerge Magazine*, *failbetter*, and *Literary Heist*, and *The Guardian*. He owes his inspiration to his mother, his brothers, and to the love of his life, Olivia.

Microplastics Could Be

By

Morris McCorvey

"Microplastics could be floating everywhere,"
The earnest reporter reported, incredulously.
She might have been the only one surprised.
More and more,
The News is less and less
New.
I mean, did you,
My teary eyed, snotnosed compadre
Need to be told?
We are constantly trading this for that?
And this aint really where it's at.
Hell,
The windblown pollen
Of genetically engineered corn
Is killing off the Monarch Butterfly
In North America!
Microplastics damned well are floating everywhere.
And, that ain't the worst of it.
But, I suppose the real news
need be broken gradually,
Kinda… slow.
Between advertisements for how to divest ourselves
of all we have
before it's time to go.

Spelled Backwards Is
(According to The Last Poets)

By

Morris McCorvey

That dog on the hill
Alone there perfectly still
Not simply watching
Observing,
My autumn commute between little theater director
And domestic inadequacy.
As I am observing a coyote carcass dissolve into the
Osage Hills.
Blending into the landscape, leaving only a skeletal
framework
Of bleached bones, over the weeks,
To be unearthed in centuries by some clever
Archaeologist who will ID them as 21st century coyote
bones.
One day, I notice that I haven't noticed them in a while.
They're just gone.
But, I was alone, driving thru those haunted hills.
So, were they ever actually there?
Driving home thru the hills one night,
I saw a small group of deer staring into my headlights
become people,
Who turned and fled up into the fall foliage,
and disappeared.
No one was along for the ride, to whom to say
"Oh,wow!"
Now,
30 years later,

film makers haunt those hills.
Ain't no telling what they will see up there.
Last night, standing in our parking lot,
I saw a comet streak right down out of the sky,
With a tail of brilliant white, green and blue.
Looked as if it might have hit the earth
somewhere near Ft. Worth.
But, I,
I was all alone.

Morris McCorvey, whose haunting voice and enchanted verse will have you saying, "Eat your heart out, Morgan Freeman" served as an artist-in-residence in schools for the Oklahoma Arts Council for almost nine years. He has been executive director of the Westside Community Center for fifteen years.

(https://emerge-writerscolony.org/author/morris-mc-corvey)

Moonbeams and Waterfalls

By

Deepa Thomas Davy

Come away with me
To splash in the puddles
To dance in the rain
To paint in the air with fingertips vain

Come away with me to an island
Where there's only you and me

Come away with me for a while
To trace imagination with our eyes

The sky will be our ceiling
The sun our warmth

The night sky our soothing blanket
The crystal stars our lights

The tinkle of the waterfall our music
And moon beams our lamps

The roar of the river
The rustle of the leaves
And the breeze
Our tender lullabies

Deepa Thomas Davy has served many years as an educator. Her academic credentials include three undergraduate degrees. After several years of enriching work experience in the field of education, she was inspired to further her own studies and succeeded in earning her postgraduate degree in English Language and Literature.

Deepa discovered the joy of writing some years ago. She finds freedom in writing and creating her own work and is currently working on her own book of poems. She finds the experience of putting thoughts into expression, both refreshing and rejuvenating. Her main inspiration comes from nature and she is drawn to its ethereal beauty. She believes in appreciating the simple joys of life, living in the present and cherishing each moment.

Website: http://sprinkledpoetry.wordpress.com

Silence

By

Kenneth Weene

I carried my toy cannon everywhere.
Fired it shouting *bang* and *boom*.
Built a fort from cushions and waited
to defend my grandfather
against the advancing German army.

Adults whispered about the Shoah.
The great wind sweeping Europe
Leaving us Jews without a Golam.

Only one demon allowed at a time
in this world

goose-stepping our relatives into camps

What kind of wind kills Jews?
Why doesn't god intervene?
Either god has no ears
    or...
        just doesn't listen to Jewish prayers.

My mother, fearful of the world,
        locked me on the porch;
The railing too high to be seen,
        too high for me to see.
I sat in a corner and crayoned rage

until the wasp attack raised my screams.

> Did the kinder of Europe scream?
> Did they have toy guns and pillow
> fortresses?
>
> Had they lived, would they
> have been overprotected by mothers
> who took their toy guns as my mother
> had taken mine?
>
> *Too much violence.*

When my uncle brought us
to the Watertown Arsenal
to see great guns being made,
I remembered my toy.

My cousin wailed in fright.
Was it those monstrous weapons,
Or the bangs and booms of machines,
Or the knowledge that it could happen
that terrified him?

In school we learned cursive
Were told to hide under desks
When we heard the bomb,
Saw the blinding light.

> Our family never talked about the wind,
> the camps. Never mentioned God.
>
> The buried can no longer be ignored.

A toy cannon screams against the wind.

He wrote to defy the guards and challenge the gods

By

Kenneth Weene

the prisoner in his flimsy striped suit
and flip-flop shoes used a mix of urine
and frass on bits of paper salvaged from the wind
blown from the city to the east
where he had lived, where his ghost
might someday haunt. He wrote with a stick
sharpened and dipped in the greenish liquid,
non-ink. Blowing to dry the simple,
squiggled words of his day spent yearning
for a glimpse, for a listening ear,
for a quick embrace.
Words stuffed into the lice and bed-bug
mattress straw to be burned on the day of release,
when the priest, dressed in white,
would absolve his sins.

Posthumous pardon offers no reprieve
to his children who'll receive
a formal certificate which again
brings tears. Such letters resurrect
the dead so mourners can remember and weep.
No parole, just permission to recall the undead,

permission to let him go.

        My Gap-dressed grandson splashed
        in the wavelets and chased snipe
        with *wahoo* and *watch me*.
        He laughed as the birds hopped about;
        then into the air, a half-eaten snail dripping
        from one mouth, a frenzy of guano from
        another orifice. The whir; wings beating
        frantic escape. *Hop-it, Hop-it* they called
        in fright. What made him, only five, a
        torturer? Is it humanity at our worst?

        In school they bullied him for his lazy eye and
        called him names to blindside him
        on the jungle gym. He no longer wanted
        to go to the park. Brooding, he'd throw
        his Thomas tank engine across the room.
        I don't care became his favorite words. About
        himself or others, who can say?

The burial pits were filled with those too weary,
those who could not climb back to the surface.
Drowning on land with sand and soil the last
breath untaken the last sound un-sighed.
He is there and the bits of paper turned
to ash and black smoke. We do not have
a pope, only the dead. Sprinkled lime
and the odor remains.
Half a day's work, the satisfied guards
march back to their barracks,
then to lunch. They drink a beer
and laugh at him;
his last desperate struggle
met with a shovel. *Did he bleed?*

Like a pig. They eat ham and cabbage.
The prisoners who live
receive cabbage soup. Perhaps today
they will find a leaf.

Novelist, short story author, and poet Kenneth Weene loves the sound and rhythm of words. A Broody New Englander by upbringing and nature, Ken focuses much of his writing on the dark side of humanity. Yet, he also celebrates the courage that allows us to persevere in the face of darkness, to deal with that which is painful. You can find more about Ken and his work at:

www.kennethweene.com

The Old Woman

By

Woody Barlow

The old woman struggled to breathe in the cold night air. Her faint breath dissipated in small white clouds above her lips, as she stared up at the stars shining in the crisp night air. *Beauty can be cruel*, she thought. The thin cardboard mattress beneath her, repurposed from a discarded Food 4 Less fruit box, and her threadbare coat provided little comfort or warmth from the cold radiating up from the brick alley. She had not eaten in days, but it didn't matter. Her sense of smell and taste were gone. She urinated where she lay shivering. The beat-up green Dumpster beside her served as a pitiful shield against the cold wind that whipped down the alley. She thought the Dumpster might contain something edible for Buddy, her wirehaired terrier, but she was too weak to get up and look. He shook constantly beneath her coat, but would not leave her to look for food.

Nancy tried to pull her fingers through her hair, but it was too tangled and matted to allow her fingers to pass. *I was beautiful once*, she thought. *Popular in school ... a cheerleader. What happened?* But, she knew the answer, as well as what the night might bring. Her mind never failed to provide life's ugly details in an unending feedback loop. First, there was the divorce from her college jock husband, Dave, who was now a successful insurance salesman. He never got over being a big man on campus, and he spent more time in front of the mirror than she did. With all his self-pampering she should have known he had a girlfriend. *How foolish of me,* Nancy thought. *Unseated by another cheerleader with more bounce.* There was no sudden-death playoff for their marriage, only the silence of unspoken words and lost emotions. Then came the crushing loneliness, set aside by two kids that needed to be raised. Medical bills piled up from her daughter's braces, and later for her son's heart valve. Dave was no help with the bills. He had a new, young wife and didn't want to be bothered with his past life.

When the kids graduated from high school and left for college, they never came back. Neither bothered to call on special occasions. Nancy knew she should have kept her mouth shut about Dave, and let go of her hatred. It was another one of life's lessons learned too late.

Alcohol became her only lover; a mercy killing one shot at a time. One day while she was floating on the river of alcoholic dreams and desolation, a registered letter came in the mail. It said the bank was repossessing her home. She threw the letter in the trash just as she had done with all the other bills. She never really wanted to deal with all the paperwork. That had been Dave's job. She allowed herself to believe that someone would come into her life, and correct the financial mess she had made for herself. Those thoughts turned out to be of little use when the

Cooper County Deputy Sheriff came knocking on the door with a handful of official looking papers. Nancy heard him say he was there for a forced eviction. The deputy tried to explain everything, but she couldn't make herself listen, or care. She looked out through the dirty, spotted front window, while ignoring the deputy standing there in his starched uniform, smelling of cheap cologne. Outside, the neighborhood kids were playing kick ball in the street. *My new home*, she mused.

Nancy stayed in cheap hotels while the money lasted. Sneaking Buddy into the room at night after she was settled in. The child support had long since dried up. She had some meager savings, and some social security income, but not enough to keep up with weekly rent payments.

In the beginning a few sympathetic friends stayed in touch and tried to help, but they had quit calling long before the deputy arrived with all those papers When what little money she had ran out, and she could no longer afford to pay the rent, Nancy washed herself and brushed her teeth in the Ladies' bathroom at McDonalds, in a last ditch effort to look presentable in case she ran into a friend, or an old acquaintance. She wondered if that was where she caught COVID-19, but it didn't matter. The state had not prioritized the homeless for vaccinations, so trying to stay clear of the unvaccinated was an impossible task.

Nancy's first symptoms were a loss of smell and taste. Then came the headaches and chills. She felt really bad for two or three days, before feeling better. But soon, the

COVID symptoms came back, and it wasn't long before she had difficulty breathing. Nancy couldn't remember how long she had been sick; time was meaningless on the street.

While she had the strength, Nancy wandered from Dumpster to Dumpster, exhaust fan to exhaust fan with Buddy, searching for food, and a warm place to hang out. Long before she became sick, Nancy had given up on shelters. They did not allow pets of any kind, and she would not part with Buddy for a meal and a night's sleep. Shelters were dangerous places anyway, there were manipulations of every kind, all under the guise of Christian fellowship. Nancy knew there would be no religious conversion for her. She and Buddy were better off living on the street eating discarded, half eaten hamburgers, and cold Chinese food salvaged from Dumpsters. Her sole purpose in life was reduced to caring for Buddy, day after freezing day.

Now she could no longer rise, or feed herself, and she had nowhere to go, and no one to turn to. The heat from fresh urine warmed her legs for a few moments. Nancy pulled Buddy tight to her chest and gave him a hug as her last breath escaped into the cold night air.

Sometime later, two men walked by the alley. One said, "Bob, let's call it a night. Christmas Parade, or no, it's too cold to hang around out here."

Bob shook his head. "I agree. Jeez, look over there."

"Where?"

"On the other side of that Dumpster. It looks like a pair of legs."

"Let's have a look," Bob said, holding back slightly.

Tom knelt down over the woman and pulled her jacket apart to check her pulse. He felt her arm for some sign of life, but there was none. "Call 911," he said.

While Bob called 911, Tom searched the old woman's pockets for some form of ID. He could only imagine her story. It was easy to see she had been beautiful once. A small picture of two school aged children in one of her pockets seemed out of place. *Where were they when she needed them?* Tom wondered. In her right hand was a rough scribbled note on a white cardboard lid used to seal Chinese food boxes. He pulled out his car keys with a small light attached, and shined it on the note. It read: please take care of Buddy. He's all I have in the world.

Tom didn't know what to make of the note until the head of a small dog popped out from inside her coat. Tom stuck out his arms. "Come here Buddy, your mom has to make the next journey by herself." He took off his jacket and cradled Buddy next to his chest to warm him, as he rubbed Buddy's head affectionately. "Your mom loved you with all her heart, and asked me to take care of you."

Bob looked down at Tom and said, "The ambulance is on the way. "What you got there?"

Tom hugged Buddy and said, "Bob, meet our newest family member, Buddy."

Woody Barlow was born in Kansas City, Missouri, and raised in Olathe, Kansas. He is the author of *Tarzan Wore Chaps*, *The Aluminum Ballet*, and a *Voice from the Void*. His new novel, *The Guardians of Eureka Springs*, is an adventure fantasy with delightful characters and a setting in the beautiful Ozark Mountains of Arkansas.

(https:www.amazon.com/WoodyBarlow/e/BooJ7BKS06)

Little Blues *

By
Annie Klier Newcomer

Can butterflies survive the cold in Alaska?
curious children ask.

A butterfly floats too high,
bumps into a billie
sure-footed on a cliff,
then trips
on the weight
of her blue.

The world basks
with outstretched
wings, waiting
for a patch of sunlight
to find strength to go on.
The Butterfly Effect.

* These small butterflies are found on alpine tundra and
subalpine meadows throughout much of Alaska.

From Annie:

My vision is that no matter how many missteps and no matter
where we land after this pandemic has given us its best shot,
that we find the strength to carry on. The interconnection
between Nature and People fascinates me. Thus a poem on the
Butterfly Effect.

Annie Klier Newcomer lives in Prairie Village, Kansas with her husband, David and their Aussiedoodle, Summit. She considers each her Muse. Volunteering at Turning Point, a Center for Hope & Healing, is a passion for her. She also coaches in Chess After-School programs in Kansas City, Missouri. An advocate for people who may not always have a voice that is loud enough to be heard, she isn't afraid to raise her own. Her work has been published in Central US, Oregon, California as well as in Great Britain, New Zealand, Australia, and Uruguay.

Life

By

Jim Young

come, sit with me
let yourself simply be
plunge, if you will, to the depths of your grief.
loosen the slipknot on your weary body and ravaged soul
freeing your burdens
your anger, your pain
whatever it is that discomforts you
whatever it is you feel.

come, sit with me
open to the joy that is you
letting laughter's release unfold your Truth.
allow yourself to bask in my love for you
healing your mind, your body, your soul.
bathe in the Light of transformation
knowing that all you have to be is you
that I'm always here for you.

come, sit with me
travel with me through the universe
being open in your tranquility
mindless in your solitude
resting your thoughts and feelings here beside me
and you will come to know
yet again
that we are One.

come, sit with me
no matter what the condition or circumstance
no matter what our past
it is safe now.
in Eternal Relationship
the fullness of presence
is all that matters;
these intimate moments
become our Truth
authentic Love our bond.

Jim Young is an award winning spiritual author, poet and photographer, applying spiritual perception in all aspects of his life's calling. A ministerial graduate of the Pecos Benedictine Monastery's ecumenical school for spiritual directors and the Minister Emeritus for the Creative Life Church in Hot Springs, AR, Jim was also a co-founder and facilitator for the AR Metaphysical Society in Eureka Springs and The Aristotle Group in Hot Springs, AR. Dr. Young also served with distinction as a teacher and distinguished professor of higher education, and in a variety of leadership positions, including President of State University of New York at Potsdam and Chancellor of the University of Arkansas at Little Rock. Author of 31 spiritual books, Dr. Young is an inspirational teacher who takes participants to the threshold of their own Truth. He is available for workshops, seminars and presentations: www.theinwardway.live.

It Won't Be Today

By

Frank Hicks

The flat tire may be an omen, but I'm forty-seven years old and don't believe in that crap any more. I have customers to see and no time for this. The sedan is hard to push, especially with the flat, but I get it out of the garage onto the driveway. Even though it's only seven thirty in the morning, sweat drenches my shirt. The workmen fixing the street watch me. Just because I wear a tie doesn't mean I'm not just as tough as they are.

I change the tire as fast as I can, then head inside to wash up. The air conditioning feels cool, but there's pressure on my chest. Not the light touch of anxiety— the crushing weight of an I-beam. Full breath is impossible. Panic rises. I slump into a living room chair. Louise is still asleep in the bedroom. I can't get back up to wake her.

"Louise, wake up." Each breath harder to pull in. "*Louise*...call nine-one-one." Seconds draw long, my chest aches, the pressure closes tighter with each attempt to inhale.

Louise pulls on her robe as she rushes into the living room. "What? What's wrong?" Her voice is sharp with fear.

I grip my chest, gasping for air. "Heart attack. Nine-one-one."

She dials, then pleads with the operator, "Please, come quick."

Immobilizing pain. Shallow, impossible breaths.

"They're coming," Louise says, kneeling next to the chair, tears running down her cheeks. "What can I do to help you?"

Unable to speak, I shake my head. A siren wails in the distance. I realize t's coming for me. The sound increases, then abruptly stops.

Two paramedics rush through the front door. One puts an oxygen mask over my nose and mouth. "What's your name? Can you tell me what it feels like?" He stabs a vein in my hand and starts an IV. The other readies the stretcher.

The presence of medical help calms me enough to be able to speak. "Can't breathe. Flat tire. Glad you're here." I don't mention rushing to change the tire, to show the workmen I was still tough. I feel stupid that I worry about stuff like that.

"The pressure you feel is, most likely, a heart attack. But help is close. Hang tough." The EMT's relaxed confidence diffuses my panic. I always worry about everything, but at that moment the effort to breathe takes all my attention.

The EMT's strap me to a gurney, then push me to the street and load me into the ambulance. The men fixing the street stop and stare. I would too. There's a real live crisis unfolding. I don't feel so tough any more. Breathing is all but impossible. I am embarrassed to be on this stretcher, helpless.

One EMT sits in back with me, watching the numbers on a machine I am hooked up to, talking to someone (at the hospital, I think), and affirming to me I am doing okay.

We get to the hospital fast. The surroundings fade. I am eased gently onto a table. Nurses pull off my clothes.

Louise watches, red-faced, tears streaming down.

"Stop crying," I bark. "I can't stand you crying."

She jerks back like I've punched her, then sniffles and covers her face. I am irritated at her. I'm the one having a heart attack. She needs to buck up.

Nurses and doctors slide me back onto a gurney. A man pushes the stretcher through a series of halls. A young woman in surgical garb walks alongside, gently stroking my forehead. She doesn't speak, but her gentle touch is ripe with kindness. I am deeply comforted by her gesture. I still feel like I cannot breathe, but I am no longer angry or afraid.

The ceiling floats by above me, when suddenly, my vision goes completely black. I have not passed out. The touch of the young woman continues to calm me, yet, even with my eyes open, I see only darkness. Seconds later, as suddenly as the dark appeared, pure white light fills my field of vision. This is not blinding light, not a flash, rather all-encompassing light. After a few seconds the light disappears. I see the ceiling again sailing by above me. In that instant I realize I may die, but then, I may not. I'm okay with not knowing, aware I have no control at this point anyway. This calm acceptance is unfamiliar to me.

The cath lab is dimly lit. A small army, dressed in surgical garb, attend to instruments. I am awake as the surgeon threads a catheter from my groin toward the blocked artery. A screen shows a real-time picture of my heart. A few veins, white with radioactive dye, stand out on a field of black. Sharp pain squeezes my chest as the balloon on the end of the catheter is inflated, stopping blood flow. The balloon deflates and pain subsides. The screen lights up with a maze of veins as the dye is borne to places in my heart that were blocked off by years of neglect and bad decisions.

I am stripped of pretension. My life comes down to an instrument repairing, in moments, damage done gradually over time. Darkness has become light. Life is reaching parts of me that were previously starved of connection. I am awed at what a gift this is. And then, I sleep.

I wake up in the ICU. Louise is here. So are Tim and Marci, our children. We hug, we talk. I tell them about the moments of darkness and light for which I have no explanation. And about the young lady, whose touch was so remarkable. I tell them how baffled I am by these experiences, and yet comforted.

All is well until intense pain, like a vise, clamps my heart again. I grab my chest and roll onto my side.

Louise runs to the door. "Help! Somebody, come!"

A nurse rushes in and gives me a tiny pill. "Put this under your tongue." She turns to Louise. "It's angina. The nitroglycerin will stop the pain."

Louise hugs our daughter. The nurse stands at the bedside and watches me.

Sounds drift away. I feel comfortable and sleepy and without a care. Everything fades to black until... nothing.

Voices from a distance. "Mr. Hicks. Mr. Hicks. Wake up, Mr. Hicks."

I rise out of a mental down comforter. Doctors and nurses surround the bed. Someone is pushing a milky liquid into the IV line. An oxygen mask covers my mouth and nose again. "What happened?" I ask.

"You reacted to the nitro. It's not common, but it happens."

Louise is crying again. "I don't want him to die."

The nurse hugs her. "Oh hon, he's gonna die, but it won't be today." Her matter-of-fact comment is the perfect response to Louise's fear, and I laugh out loud. Dying isn't funny, but having come so close and escaping makes the moment rich. I embrace this moment, aware that it is the only one I have for sure.

The author resides in Waldport, OR where he walks on the beach most days and finds more inspiration than sea glass or beautiful shells. His first novel, *The Long Ride: Learning About Life From an Outlaw Biker* was published in 2019 by Black Rose Writing. His poetry, memoir and fiction have been published in *Ariel Chart* and *Emerge Magazine* as well as various anthologies.

The Promise

By

Dot Hatfield

Does God forgive broken promises?

Angie pondered this thought as her finger idly traced the scar on her wrist. *Will God understand that sometimes we say we'll do something and when the time comes we just can't?*

Of course, Dr. B. took issue with the word "can't." She always said, "Maybe you can't sing. You probably can't fly. But, you can pick up a phone."

"That is true," Angie said aloud. The bathtub full of water gave her voice resonance. "I can make the call. But, I don't want to. I'm afraid of interference."

She couldn't take a chance on someone stopping her. Gail was gone this weekend. Angie should do it while she had the place to herself.

Earlier today, when she picked up the mail, the official envelope from the State Pardon and Parole Board caught her eye immediately. She stared at the unopened letter lying among the stack of Christmas cards. She knew what it said.

"The offender in your case will be reviewed for parole … you have the right to appear … make a statement …."

He's up for parole, and I'm still in prison.

Holding the envelope, she climbed out the window onto the fire escape, three stories above the street. She sucked the cold air into her lungs, hoping to clear her mind. Her thin jacket gave little protection from the icy wind as she leaned against the frozen wrought iron banister that framed the landing. Removing the letter from the envelope, she tore it in half – and half again – and again, as many times as she could. Opening her hand, she watched the bits of white paper float away in the frigid updraft of the alley beside the building.

Dr. B. says it's time I took charge of my own life. If I want closure, it's up to me to do something about it.

By the time she re-entered the warmth of the apartment, she had a plan.

After Gail left on her weekend ski trip, Angie decorated the little tree. She hung lights and a few ornaments on the scrawny branches and topped it off with the homemade aluminum foil star. The radio provided music of the season while she addressed her few cards, adding personal notes to some of them.

These preparations finished, she soaked herself in deep, luxurious foam. Bubble baths were a nightly ritual, known for helping soothe, comfort and calm frayed emotions.

Angie pulled the plug and stepped out onto the mat. It felt sticky with hair spray, so she quickly found her slippers, toweled herself dry and put on her robe. The last of the water drained away; scented foam lay in a heap under the perpetual drip of the faucet.

For a moment, the gaunt face looking back from the mirror startled her. The puffy dark eyes witnessed to

158

nights without sleep. She opened the medicine cabinet and the image went away.

Okay. I've been soothed by bubbles. Now, I will calmly take about twenty sleeping pills.

She lifted the bottle from the shelf and walked through the apartment she shared with her cousin. After Angie lost her job, Gail had taken her in. During the months that followed, when Angie could not work, Gail had been supportive, encouraging her to seek counseling. Every little bit of progress she had made, Gail had been right there with her.

She'll be glad for this to be over, too.

Seated at the kitchen table, Angie dumped out the capsules. She meticulously placed them in a neat row, the red end on top, the yellow on bottom. She rearranged them, lined them up end to end, alternated colors, made checkerboard designs.

"Let's see," she said aloud, "Do I want to chase them with water or something a bit stronger?" Vodka would be more lethal, if she could keep it down. But, if she threw up ....

Water, then. She picked a bottle of Aquafina from the fridge.

Everything ready, she thought again of The Promise. How many people had she made that contract with, anyway? Dr. B., Gail, the nurse in the E.R., the counselor on the crisis line .... Every imaginable euphemistic phrase had been used: when you're depressed, feel alone, think you can't go on, want to hurt yourself, yada, yada, yada. But they all meant the same thing. Before you pull that

159

trigger, take those pills, jump off a bridge or slash your wrists – promise, before you commit suicide, you will talk it over with someone.

If I tell them, they'll send me to the hospital. Or, at the very least, insist on another contract. I suppose I could take the pills and then call. But I promised to call before.

She dialed the number on the card taped to the telephone and held the receiver to her ear. As the first ring ended, panic gripped her. She slammed the phone down before anyone could answer.

No! I'm not ready! I don't want to talk about it! Promise be damned!

A flashing memory came to her. One terrible night that changed the course of her life. She should have locked the car. Even those few minutes while she paid for gas. Enough time for him to slip into the back seat.

The volunteer who came to the hospital gave her Dr. B.'s card. But, she didn't see the doctor right away. Not until Mark left, saying she needed to "let it go, already." Not until her boss told her to take a leave of absence and pull herself together. Not until Gail found her lying in the bathroom, her wrists bleeding from the razor cut.

Once more, she touched the scar. Was what happened her fault? Or God's cruel way of getting even? Months of counseling. Still looking for answers.

Then, the trial. She had to tell – relive – everything he did. Trembling in the witness chair, while he sat at a table ten feet away, she listened numbly while the defense attorney attacked her character.

Since that time, she had faced squarely the question of

whether she had the right to take her own life. She believed God wanted her to live in the best way she could – but, she also believed God gave her the right to turn out the light when life no longer had meaning.

I'm trying to be responsible. Gail would find her, but the scene would not be too horrible. Nothing like before.

Dr. B. often said that Angie had come a long way in her journey to healing. Each step she took – steeled herself to take – brought the whole incident that much closer to being over.

It will never be over. He got 15 years. My sentence is for life.

She stood. The room tilted, then rocked. Her heart pounded in her ears. With every beat, the pain in her chest grew sharper. She gasped, lowered herself to the floor and curled up in a fetal position. The loose robe fell open, exposing the thin body to the stark overhead light. With eyes closed tightly, she concentrated on breathing slowly, deliberately. Inhale-two-three-four; exhale-two-three-four.

After a few minutes, her breath came normally and her pulse slowed. She became aware of her surroundings: the cold linoleum, the soft whir of the electric clock, the blinking Christmas lights in the next room. She lay there, experiencing a strange feeling of accomplishment at having managed the episode alone. Dr. B. would say, "I'm proud of you. You are very brave."

Facing a panic attack does take courage, I suppose. She sat up and wiped her face on the end of her robe. *And it will take guts to swallow a handful of pills and fall asleep, knowing I'll never wake up. So, which is braver? To live with the pain, or to die and stand before God with a broken promise on my soul?*

She pulled herself into the chair and took a long drink from the bottle of water on the table. To die or to live?

Her finger touched the redial button. A voice interrupted the second ring, "Crisis Line, may I help you?" Angie took a deep breath.

"Yes – I – promised I would call."

Dot Hatfield lives in Beebe, Arkansas and is the 2020 Inductee to the Arkansas Writers' Hall of Fame.

Who Would Have Guessed?
A true story

By

Julie Peterson Freeman

On a Friday, January 13th 1950, we were braving a huge snowstorm on the way to the hospital when I came out of my mom wearing tap shoes and singing "On The Good Ship Lollipop." Well not really, but almost. Anyway, I made it into this world.

Lying in front of the pecan Hi-Fidelity cabinet with the straight pointed legs in my home at 4014 Sheridan South, I waited for my mommy to set up the ironing board, plug in the iron, and carefully place the 33 ⅓ LP on the spindle so we could sing and dance to Shirley Temple's songs from the movies we adored and watched over and over again.

In the 1930's when she was a little girl, Mommy watched her Shirley Temple movies at the movie theater five blocks away from her home. It only cost a nickel. My sisters and I watched those same movies on the television in our living room. Heck, even my little brothers watched *Captain January*, *The Little Colonel*, and *Rebecca of Sunnybrook Farm* as those boys were good singers and dancers, too.

In 1957, Mommy asked me what I wanted from Santa for Christmas. The sole thing on my list was a 12" Shirley

Temple Doll—the least expensive one. I figured if I asked for only one thing, and if it was affordable, my chances of getting what I really wanted would improve. And it worked! Christmas morning, smiling up at me, there she was lying under the Christmas tree in her pink onesie with my name attached to her wrist—my very own 12" vinyl Shirley Temple doll. Oh, how I cherished that doll.

The years passed, life's desires took hold of me, and along the way my beloved Shirley Temple doll fell by the wayside. I looked high and low for her, but I couldn't find her anywhere. Well into my 30's, I was at a loss to find Shirley no matter how hard I tried. Although she won't admit it, I think my mom put her in a box to give to the Good Will, poor baby.

I had to find her. That's all there was to it. I scoured every antique shop I happened upon, but not one Shirley Temple doll peaked out through the glass cases.

One evening, I had a good hour before my French class was to begin at the Alliance Francaises located in the warehouse district of downtown Minneapolis, so I decided to order a frothy cappuccino at the nearby bookstore. There was an antique shop next door, so after drinking my coffee, I gave finding my 50's Shirley another try. And there she was sitting all pert and pretty in a foggy glass case near the back. I'm telling you, that Shirley doll was smiling at me. I convinced myself she was indeed my long lost doll from my childhood. Ninety-five dollars later, she was once again resting safely in my loving arms.

As a child, many Sunday mornings were spent sitting on my daddy's lap combing over the want ads of the hefty five inch thick Minneapolis Star/Tribune. If there was something to be had at a darn good price, you could find it among the hundreds of little boxes advertising used cars, ebony clarinets, and washer/dryer combinations. So, when the internet hit, it hit me hard. Obsessively hard. Ebay was pure magic. I set my alarm for the middle of night to get in on a last minute bid for a ruby and gold pagoda ring listed in Thailand. It was beyond amazing. You could buy a 1,000 year-old enameled cricket cage from China and Civil War daguerreotypes in hard cases. I bought a 1963 Morris Minor 1000 right hand drive stick shift with a big white steering wheel out of the UK. After six months, I managed to get Petula through Homeland Security and into my garage. One day I set about finding a 1930's 13" composition Shirley Temple doll like the one my mom would have had when she was a little girl. It was easy, but it was also expensive. Still, the one I found and purchased was in very good shape for being so old.

Surprisingly, my mom passed on keeping the 13" composition Shirley Temple doll she would have had as a child, so I decided to post her for sale on Ebay for twice what I paid for her. Moments later, a girl bought my 30's Shirley paying full price on a "Buy It Now." There was no doubt the buyer wanted that particular doll. I was to send Shirley in a sturdy box carefully cushioned in many layers of bubble wrap to Gina Napolitano at a shipping address in the Rossville neighborhood of Staten Island, NY. Gina was over the top excited about her purchase and once you hear her story you will be, too. Gina couldn't spill the beans to her mama, so she exploded with her plans in an Ebay message to me

"I'm going to take a composition doll restoration class and make that old Shirley Temple doll brand spanking new again," explained Gina. "You see," Gina went on, "my mother grew up in the poorest Italian neighborhood on Staten Island. When the Depression hit her family, it flattened them with a black asphalt stench and the total annihilation of a double drum road roller." (Note: I delighted in what I knew was Gina's Italian/NYC accent crawling out from behind every syllable of her writing.) "Mama was a little girl when the Depression robbed people of what it means to be human." wrote Gina. My mama's parents, my grandmama and grandpapa, wouldn't let my mama play with her Shirley doll because if she broke it, they would not be able to buy her another one. So, they boxed up Mama's Shirley and put her high on a shelf in the back of a closet for safe keeping only allowing her to take the doll out at Christmas.

Mama was eight years-old and it was the long awaited Christmas Day—the day she would be allowed to play with Shirley. Mama invited her friend from next door over to play with Shirley too because her friend did not have a Shirley Temple doll of her own. Cradling her precious Shirley in her arms, Mama went to the back door to let her friend in. Mama's friend took one look at Mama's Shirley Temple doll and became enraged with jealousy. She grabbed the doll by one leg and smashed her over and over again against the wall, cracking her face, legs, and fingers beyond repair. Mama couldn't stop sobbing. That doll meant everything to her.

When Mama had me, she told me the awful story about seeing her Shirley in crumbling pieces on the kitchen floor. She told me over and over again, year after year after year, "Gina, I still miss that doll. My yearning for my Shirley never really goes away."

"Oh, my, Gina," I wrote back. "This is so heartfelt and good; it might be the most amazing Christmas present ever. Gina, I have *Rebecca of Sunnybrook Farm* bib overalls and a straw hat for that doll that I want to give to your mom, okay? In fact, I have an original Baby Take a Bow dress I will send to you as well. Would that be okay?" I asked.

"Absolutely," Gina wrote. "This is going to be even better than I imagined. "I'd better get on with the lessons and restoration," Gina wrote. "Christmas is in two months, and I want Shirley to be perfect."

Six weeks passed and I'd heard nothing from Gina until one day I received a message with a photo attached. Gina had worked magic into the composition of that 1930's doll. If you looked long and hard enough the smile on Shirley's face became real. Shirley's golden curls were divine.

On Christmas Day, I received a note from Gina with a video attached. In the video, Gina's mama sat in a chair waiting for Gina to give her her Christmas present. Gina placed a beautifully wrapped box on her mama's lap. Gina's papa took the video of Mama unwrapping her gift. When Gina's mama removed the lid, she gasped, "My doll. My doll. You've come back to me. My doll." Mama looked up into Gina's face with a look for which words can never do justice. Silence took over the room except for nose blowing and tears. Mama held her long lost Shirley Temple doll to her shoulder cooing and kissing her face.

And a thousand miles away, a stranger who sold an old doll on Ebay cried.

Gina wrote one last thing to me before signing off:

"Thank you, Julie. If you ever decide to come to Rossville on Staten Island, come and visit us. We'll walk down to Portofino Pizza for a slice, my treat. I promise you will not be disappointed. Porofino's is a small family owned pizzeria that also has fresh garlic knots that are out of this world.

Merry Christmas with love, Gina Napolitano."

Julie Peterson Freeman, née Wren Dubois, has been spotted in dark piano bars and tiny cafes in the oldest sections of cities around the world. It was in Paris that the figure of the flâneur was created, the prototypical individual who wanders the labyrinthine urban sprawl, a nimble observer of life. Bien sûr, none of this is true, except in Julie's imagination.

Twinkle! Twinkle!

By

Aileen Bartlett

With the taste of candy apples still on our lips, we returned to school after the Halloween break. In those days, every year flew by in a flash and 1983 was no exception. Autumn Nature Tables filled with orangey-brown leaves and conkers were cleared to make way for Christmas. It was our third year in Primary School and by then, we knew the drill. Every subject for the next six weeks would revolve around the obvious theme. Our heads would be filled with images of Santa, his reindeer and his elves and our schoolbooks would be filled with festive activities. Christmas poems and stories in English lessons; Christmas Carols in music and for history we'd learn the origins of our Irish traditions and celebrations. Of course, a lot of time would be spent adding to our 'God Book'. The familiar tale of a virgin mother travelling to Bethlehem on a donkey to register her name with her betrothed seemed like old news to a class of six- and seven-year-olds, but we'd play along, listening intently, waiting for something new in the story.

In P1 and P2 we'd starred in the Nativity story in front of proud parents and grandparents who sat with tears in their eyes for reasons we couldn't comprehend. Surely, they knew the story better than we did, and it wasn't an overly sad story to elicit tears. Each class performed their Christmas play, which meant the audience had to sit through six different versions of the same nativity.

'It's a girl,' one of the Joseph's called out from the stage, leading to uproarious laughter from the audience and a spontaneous flood of tears from the five-year-old Mary who had brought a blue blanket to wrap her infant child.

'Can I be Mary this year Miss?' I asked our P3 teacher.

I thought if I made it clear I was ready for the lead role, Miss McCartan would be over the moon not to have to sit through fifteen auditions.

'We're not doing the Nativity this year, Amy,' she told me.

'What are we doing instead, Miss?'

'It's a surprise. Now go sit down and we'll talk about it after Maths.'

I couldn't concentrate on 'The Story of 9' and didn't even appreciate the Christmas themed handout complete with elves and cookies. My mind was filled with ideas about the play. What could we be doing?

Our Catherine had told me not to expect a Nativity, but she was a know-it-all, and I didn't half believe her.

'Sure, we did Santa's Workshop in P3. Remember? I was the lead.'

'You were not. You were Mrs Claus.'

'And Mrs Claus is the female lead,' she sniffed.

I hadn't the energy to take the bait for an argument. Besides, I didn't want to be Mrs Claus. I couldn't stand being critiqued on my performance by my eight-year-old sister. I could just imagine her lifting her nose in the air as she put me down.

'Well Mr Maguire said I was better than you. He said he'd never seen a more convincing Mrs Claus in his whole life.'

I decided to ask if I could be the head elf if we were doing something about Santa's workshop. Peter would definitely be Santa Claus, because of his confidence and obvious stage presence. His best friend, Damien would have the second highest role for a boy. It wasn't like he would speak on stage, but his Dad was a teacher in the school, and he had to be front and centre. Eva was the most confident girl, so she could be Mrs Claus. The rest of us could be elves and I would be their leader. That settled I was able to give some of my time to the number nine.

In the afternoon, we listened to the story of the Angel Gabriel appearing to Mary and we coloured in a picture of Mary kneeling in prayer in front of a very friendly looking Angel.

'Right, everyone put your books away. We're going to learn a new song this afternoon.'

Christmas Carols in November. The butterflies engulfed my tummy as I thought about our play and Christmas and Santa. My books away, I sat up nice and straight and smiled up at Miss McCartan. This audition was starting now. I'd make sure she could hear my singing, even though our table was at the back of the room. Mammy had once told me I had a lovely singing voice. It was the best compliment I ever received. Especially since

Mammy had an amazing voice and sang at all the weddings and funerals in the parish.

'I've got our new song on tape and I'm going to put the words on the board,' Miss told us. She switched on the overhead projector and put the acetate film on the glass top.

'Miss, it's upside-down,' Eva called out.

'Silly me. Just let me hit play and I'll…'

In a flash she pressed the play button and stood in front of the projector to turn over the lyrics.

I didn't recognise the intro, and it didn't sound like one of the Carols I knew.

'Miss, we can't see,' Sarah McGlinchey snorted a laugh from across the room.

'Sorry. Sorry. I'll sit,' Miss McCartan sat down.

I looked back at the board and read the first line of the lyrics. 'Robin Hood, Robin Hood. Riding through the glen!'

What was this? This wasn't very Christmasy. We sat in silence listening to the chirpy song. Kyle and Michael were dancing and pulling faces to get attention from everyone, until the teacher scowled at them.

We listened to the song again and just before the bell rang at the end of the day, Miss McCartan filled in the blanks.

'Miss Murray's class will be doing a play about Santa's workshop, and I've decided we'll do Robin Hood and his Merry Men.'

My heart sank. All the lead roles would be for the boys. Peter would be Robin Hood for sure and Damien would be Little John. There were only seven more boys in our class, and I was sure they'd be the Merry Men.

Out of nowhere, Miss McCartan asked, 'Was anyone a flower-girl this year?'

My hand shot up in the air and as I looked around the room, it was clear I was the only one who had a starring role at a summer wedding.

'Great, Amy. Do you still have your bouquet?'

'Yes Miss,' I said excitedly.

'Well, ask your Mum if you can bring it in for the play.'

The bell rang and once I had my chair on top of my desk, I ran to the cloakroom to get my coat. I rushed home ahead of my sister and two brothers. I had to have Mammy's full attention before the others got home. Puffed out, I struggled to get a breath when I reached the front door.

'Where's the rest of them?' Mammy asked.

'They were too slow. I had to tell you…'

'Did something happen? Is something wrong?'

'Yes. I mean, 'No.' Nothing bad. Miss said we're doing Robin Hood for our play, and she wants me to bring in my bouquet from Auntie Jen's wedding.'

'For Robin Hood?'

'Yes. We're doing the wedding. Maid Marian and Robin,' I blurted. 'Miss might let me be Maid Marian if I bring in my bouquet.'

'She might not.'

'But I'm the only one with a bouquet.'

I was delighted when Mammy said I could bring my bouquet into school, and I spent the hours before bed imagining my role in the play.

'Mammy, can I tell Miss I can wear Catherine's Communion dress for the wedding dress?'

'Only if she's really stuck for a costume,' Mammy said reluctantly.

'Thanks Mammy. I'm gonna be the most beautiful bride.'

At breakfast, I looked at the pink and white artificial flowers in my bouquet and once I'd finished my cereal, I carefully put my bouquet into a plastic bag. I carried the bag with pride the whole way to school, along the corridor and into the classroom.

I was beside myself with excitement and was eager to show the bouquet to Miss McCartan. I must admit I was a little deflated when she dismissed me and said I'd have to wait until the afternoon for rehearsals to show her the bouquet.

Throughout the day, I struggled to contain myself and imagined myself on stage wearing Catherine's Communion dress, holding my own bouquet, and standing beside Peter as Robin Hood. I rushed back to class after the lunch break and carefully removed the artificial flowers from the carrier bag.

'Can I see it?' Eva asked. 'It's so pretty.'

'I want to be Maid Marian,' I confided.

'I can be your lady-in-waiting,' Eva laughed.

Miss McCartan settled the class as she set up the tape recorder and the over-head projector.

'I've decided we don't really have time for auditions, and so I've assigned the parts for everyone in the play.

174

Amy has been very kind to bring in her bouquet for the wedding scene.'

I beamed a smile across the room at the teacher and raised my hand to speak.

'Just a second Amy. I want to read out the parts first. Peter will be Robin Hood and Damien will be Little John. Kevin P will be Friar Tuck and Kevin H will be Will Scarlet. The rest of the boys will be Merry Men. Sarah will be Maid Marian and Claire will be her lady-in-waiting. The rest of the girls will be trees in Sherwood Forest. Oh Kyle, I need you to be the Sheriff.'

As she spoke, Miss McCartan lifted the bouquet from my desk and set it in front of Sarah.

I was devastated and bit my bottom lip to stop myself from crying. I couldn't believe the teacher would give my flowers to someone else. I looked over at Sarah McGlinchey who was flicking her hair and blowing kisses towards Peter. Claire Hughes was delighted to be centre of attention with Sarah.

'I think we'll listen to the song again and then we'll learn it line by line,' Miss McCartan said raising her voice a little over the noise.

Eva nudged me to offer support.

'Don't cry Amy. Don't let them know you're annoyed.'

I forced a half-smile at Eva.

'We'll be the best trees in Sherwood Forest,' she said trying to make me laugh.

The afternoon dragged in and when I arrived home Mammy wanted to hear all the news.

'Well, is it Maid Marian coming for tea this evening?'

'No Mammy. She gave it to Sarah McGlinchey.'

'Did Sarah bring in flowers too?'

'No, she gave her my bouquet and I have to be a tree in Sherwood Forest.'

'That'll be because her Dad's the caretaker.'

'I know and she can't even sing.'

'Well, you know what I always say, 'Don't get mad...''

'Get even?'

'Exactly,' Mammy said. 'Daddy and I will make your costume, and you are going to be the best tree on that stage.'

'That's what Eva said.'

'And Eva is one hundred per cent right,' Mammy hugged me. 'You'll get the Best Supporting Actress award if it's the last thing you do.'

And that's what I did. I practiced standing tall, swaying like a tree in a storm and smiling from ear to ear as I sang. Only Eva and my family knew how hurt I was by the casting and even though Sarah McGlinchey pulled the tiny heads of the pink and white flowers in my bouquet, I refused to react.

Mammy made me a brown skirt for my trunk, and she sewed lots of fabric leaves onto a bottle green t-shirt and Daddy made a cardboard cut-out for round my head and painted it all different shades of green.

On the day of the performance, Mammy and Daddy sat in the audience, as proud as punch. I was so happy because I had the best costume on the stage. I sang at the top of my voice and smiled and swayed in the fake breeze and shuddered when the Sheriff of Nottingham came onto the stage. Sarah McGlinchey wasn't taking it seriously at all. She kept laughing and telling everyone she couldn't remember her lines. I could see Miss McCartan in the front row, and I could tell by her face she wasn't at all happy with Sarah McGlinchey.

After the show, Peter made Sarah cry when he told her she'd ruined it for everyone with her laughing and carry-on. She ran to the classroom to get changed out of her costume with Claire chasing after her. I stayed in the hall with all the other trees and took the praise from our parents.

'You were brilliant,' Mammy said. 'Everyone's talking about you and your costume.'

'Did you get your flowers back Amy?' Miss McCartan interrupted.

'No Miss. I don't want them back. Sarah ruined them.'

'Just put them in the bin,' Daddy told her. 'We're taking Amy out for lunch to celebrate her performance. She'll see you after Christmas.'

Miss McCartan nodded as if Daddy needed permission to take me home.

'Yes. Merry Christmas Amy.

'You were brilliant today.'

'Happy Christmas Miss.'

Mammy and Daddy took me by the hand and swung me along the corridor and out to the car.

'I wonder what a tree eats for lunch,' Daddy laughed.

'Ice-cream and chocolate sauce,' I grinned chancing my arm.

'Ice-cream it is then,' Daddy said as he opened the car

door for me. 'Now that you're a big star you can't be opening your own doors.'

Aileen Bartlett is a writer and English teacher from Belfast, Ireland. To engage pupils, she wrote short and flash fiction. After researching her own family history, Aileen wrote her first novel *Buckle My Shoe* about her Grandmother Cassie and Great-Aunt Alice who grew up in Belfast during World War 1, The Easter Rising and the 1920s Troubles. *Buckle My Shoe* is available on Kindle. In August 2018, Aileen staged her first comedy play at Féile an Phobail, the West Belfast Festival. *Here's Me* is a three-hand comedy set in a Belfast bar. In August 2019, her second play, *Our Cod Reigns* debuted at Féile and was due to run under the title *Oh My Cod* in May 2020 for a 12-day run in Belfast followed by a tour of theatres in the North of Ireland. Unfortunately, this was postponed due to COVID-19. Aileen hopes this production will be scheduled again in the near future.

(https://smile.amazon.com/Aileen-Bartlett/e/)

Dear Ms. Drummon

By

Darren Chase

* * *

*

An epistolary story about two high school teenagers in the era of the First Gulf War. One of the characters is a recent Iraqi immigrant, the other a very-Californian son of hippies. Both perspectives are written by this white man in the first person, and emergent English language conventions are used to express the Iraqi boy's thoughts. While I am intimately familiar with both cultural backgrounds on a personal level, I do understand and acknowledge the problematic nature of this dynamic.

San Dieguito High School

Faruq Al-Fatir

English 12B
Period 2
My Diary Assinment

10 November 1991
This assignment is hard. I feel to write just many words and pass in. You really not reading our Diary Ms. Drummond? How is the grade then? Mother say I have to do everythings in school so I do. Mother is not happy here. She love our country. I don't know. I like my class. 12 grade is good for my eyes going out to the new things but safe there. My heart is miss my home but I am not

scare here like before in Iraq. Now different scare. I am afraid I might try all.

Many greatest wishes,

Faruq

--

17 November, 1991

Now I know how to write the Diary. You are true not reading this, just giving the happy man stamp. But you tell how to end the write so you read little bit I know this. Ok. You are good woman like my mother. Mother is whole of world for me. She teach me English in Iraq, always make English songs and books in our house, everything she have she give to children and she work all day all night, sell jewelry when we need gold for money. In here we have same family, harder the work. I don't work in Iraq. Here I am working but I like working in the chicken wheel deli. I meet Rain first day school. He talk to me first. Rain's name is mean rain like from sky. His name is like Arabic name or Turk. Most Americans names not names like Water, Kind, True. Rain name like Iran or Iraq or Turkin. Rain have different from other American. Make me smile so much. He smile so much.

Your,

Faruq

--

November 24, 1991

Last time I write Diary I write in Iraq. Every day I write what happens from war, from the beginning to when we leave to the US. So Diary is a sad thing. In the future I will to read and give the people so they know how the war happen. War was not like they say here. I tired. School and work in night very hard. Also I am like the father of my family now. I meet suitors with mother for Fatma. Now one new man, new as I here ask her marriage. I say, wait, later. He says he go to another. He have a good

family for our family but not now. Too young. Americans do not marriage young. I am father, I say no. After I talk to Rain about this because he is American. He made so funny. Say he be my wife. Funny man.
Yours,
Faruq

San Dieguito High School
                    Rain Macallan
English 12B
Period 4
Diary Assignment

November 10, 1991
Dear Dirty Dirty Dirty Little Whore Diary,
I know you read these Ms. Drummond. Get a life. No one buys your "skim without my glasses" grading policy. Whatever. At least you grade things. Jesus I tried to get a poem back from Mr. Cotter that I wrote LAST WEEK and he said he threw them out already. I was absent like the one day he returned them and so it went into the "circular file." I titled it "Plaguing Part." How can I ever write it again? It was about a part of my soul that I would hack off if I could. Depths of despair-type stuff. That was last week. What a difference a week makes.
Eat me,
Rain
--
November 17, 1991
These exercises are futile. What is nature but a dictionary said Baudelaire. I thought for a while that I could get to know myself and then I'd be more content but I found that's impossible. Yes, Ms. Drummond, "that's" refers to both the knowing and the contentment. Leah and I founded a new philosophical movement one morbidly

sunny day on the quad. We call it The File Drawer. It's very simple: You have an emotional problem, you put it in the file drawer for later and you pull it out when you're ready to deal with it, or not. In the meantime there are cigarettes. Did I mention there's a key? You've got to lock that drawer.

Yours,

Rain

--

November 24, 1991

I haven't slept a minute. We met at the beach last night really late. We walked and walked for miles talking about everything. I've never talked about everything, not even with Leah. And I listened to the person, heard so much about things I never knew or thought I could know or knew I wanted to know. I can't breathe. If I breathe I'll explode under my skin so I breathe super shallow but I want to scream. This person and I walked and walked and talked all night. I snuck in and it was daylight. Dad was taking a shower. There were plankton all down the beach last night. Our footsteps glowed like Michael Jackson in Billie Jean. They have that video in Iraq too.

Over and out,

Rain

--

1 December

Faruq

Rain is "bored." He always says he is boring. Why? He have a house, he have family, they are very strange family. Everytime music and "films," not movie they say "film." Always everyday they play piano and sing and then to dancing class. After dancing class Rain's mom buys apple juice for all girls. Many girls and Rain is only boy in dancing. Why he boring when so much happen? In

Iraq I was also dancing. Iraqi dances. I was dance one time Iraqi dancing for Saddam when I was a little boy! Now in here no dancing, only work. Maybe soon over there no Saddam. But Saddam was always love the dancing. Now maybe never dancing in Iraq.

--

December 1

Rain

I cry for no reason. I hear a song, even far away, a song I don't know, on some car radio down the street and I'm weeping. Of course we can't tell anyone. Leah would understand but even she might blab. I call him "they" whenever I talk about him.

We had no place to go last night, not my place, not his. So I took him to the bushes where the migrants sleep. He saw I was nervous but there was no time to explain. Carpet on the dirt floor, stank odor of cleome. My back pressed on the dirty carpet left by the workers. He said he'd never done it face to face. I walked him home and lay in my bed with eyes open till morning. I didn't get up to wash.

The alarm went off for school. I got up in clothes that smelled of him, stepped out into the cold without a jacket. Was on my way to the bus but didn't make it, ran back down to see the place, to make sure it had all really happened, the stinky flowers, the tunnel in the bushes, the empty corona bottles. To make sure it hadn't been a dream.

There was a car, idling close to the bushes and the driver got out. He opened all the doors and the trunk and got back into the driver's seat and people came running out of the bushes, men, women and a baby. They jumped in, and disappeared into the upholstery, or the hulk of the car, or the trunk, I don't know where, and then they were gone. The car took off. The dust settled into the dew quickly.

--

January 2

Faruq

Back the school after holiday. I am happy back in the school. Too much thinking at home. The deli closed down and only home chores to do and my mind was wild. Now I have time for boring like Rain. But Rain act like he don't know me. Now Rain always busy and he don't want to meet. Why busy? Rain don't work.

Rain give me tape before, mixed tape. Songs so strange. Not like radio music, some classic, some very strange. I listen when I think wild. Now I can listen I have time. Now I boring like Rain. I listen and end of tape, Rain is singing. Same songs as tape, only Rain, no music. Then he is smoking. I hear the smoking, think he forget to turn it off. I was breathing with him smoking. Then the tape end, click, I am sad, no reason. I hate boring.

--

January 7

Rain

Auto shop? Really auto fucking shop? No really, fuck this. Ok, it's my own goddamn fault for putting off my shop credits until now, but how could they not add me to woodworking? The dudes in auto are HARD Ms Drummond. I mean, I don't know how long I can go without a fight. Every damn day there's a melee. For real! It's like the Thunderdome in there. TWO MEN ENTER ONE MAN LEAVES. And Mr. Desnoyers doesn't seem to care. Or maybe he even likes it. Someone pleeeeeease get me out of there! You know we actually have homework? Like, I have to go home and write a two-page paper on spark plugs or whatever. Like I have to do RESEARCH for that jerkoff shop teacher who basically runs a fight club and spends most of his time on cigarette breaks! Nah, that's not it. I'm just pissed that Faruq's in there too. Awkward. After the way we left off.

184

I still can't make sense of it. We were hanging out at Stone Steps one night, where we always meet, by the streetlight that's always been out. So I go in to kiss him like, well, like I usually do, and he jerks away like I'm...I don't know. I couldn't really see his face in the dark, but I could swear it was contorted in some kind of horror or disgust.

Then he just walked down the steps as usual. Like nothing had changed. And you know what? I just followed. I walked with him. Just had a normal nightly walk, but without all the kissing. As if nothing had changed.

--

January 25

Faruq

They steal Rain's homework. Every time Ms. Drummond. Big guy just comes to Rain, takes his paper, rips off top, writes his name where Rain's name was. Rain is red. Rain have tears I know them, I saw them. He looks down, lets Raul take it. What he can do? I talk to him after. I say I will help. He so mad. Rain push me, say Fuck. But I know he will cry later.

I am ok now in the school. I am ok. I talk to people, try to have some friend. I go to Irani girl house, Sahar and they cook and I meet Sahar's parents. Like Rain parents but more cleaner. Clean house, smell always of clean. Bowls on table but no fruit. Jar for water but no water. We talk Iran Iraq war, parents and me. Another war, the another war before this war. Always war in my life. Sahar was always born here. She is just like Rain, American. She like Rain goes protest to war Iraq. Why they care about Iraq? Parents showed me picture of protest, newspaper from protest. Try to show me something. Try to show me caring. Rain parents don't caring, also don't show caring. Rain parents smoking drugs. I never tell mother this. She

185

will never let me go with Rain anytime. I hope to go to Rain house again but Rain is less my friend now.

--

February 2

Rain

Do we get credit for work we do when we're suspended? Seriously, I'd like to know what the policy is. Can I ask a question here? You see, I'm a good kid basically. I mean, think about it. I make some weird stuff in art and I got sent home once on Toga Day because you could see my ass, but really when have I ever been a discipline problem?

I can't believe Faruq did it. One moment he's just sitting there, the next he's at Raul's throat, like REALLY at his throat, like he would have cut it if I hadn't stopped him. Then Bruce gets in there. Then yet another auto shop melee ensues.

So I stabbed someone with a pencil, what the hell was I going to do, bite Bruce? That seemed tacky. The whole pencil idea just came to me. Bruce comes at Faruq and I'm like, ok, what does a guy like me do in a situation like this? And everything goes real slow all of sudden, and I'm aware of twenty juvies looking at me and Faruq like we're lunch, and I'm thinking, what's my prison crazy move gonna be? Then I remember that urban legend about the girl in detention. She's like this mousy little good girl who gets detention for the first time and so she's like totally mortified and ashamed. So, while everyone's watching, she walks to the front of the room, real deliberately, like the chick from the Adams Family, and it's all quiet of course, and she sharpens one pencil, then she sharpens another, and everyone's like, "Nerd! Why she's gotta have TWO sharpened pencils" but then she walks back to her seat, puts the points of both pencils into

186

her nostrils and, WHAM she bangs her head down on the desk, jamming them into her brain.

So that's what I thought of when I went at Bruce's back with a pencil, which, by the way, wasn't that sharp after all. And I didn't get it in that far, it just kinda pricked his shoulder blade and skidded down his back. So that's why I was so surprised when BRUCE IS CRYING ON THE FLOOR! And for some reason that really pissed me off! Like, all that time I was so afraid of him and his buddy Raul and now he's gonna sob on the floor cause I jabbed a centimeter of graphite into his shoulder blade? Fuck! So for once, I'm not crying. Actually, I'm thinking about my dad and how he cries like that, just when it's time to man up. Like when he apologized for fucking me up when I was young and I thought it meant something but then he started to cry and it was pathetic and made the apology absolutely meaningless for everyone but himself and all about forcing me to comfort him and so I just start kicking the kid. I'm kicking and kicking and he's like shielding himself but I'm cracking ribs now and Faruq's over there fucking up Raul and, strangely, all the cholos and hard-asses are like standing around NOT DOING ANYTHING. Then Mr. Desnoyers came back from his smoke break. And we're totally fucked because, despite all those weeks of teacher-sanctioned cage fighting, WE'RE the villains.

--

February 4

Faruq

Mother is very angry. She don't talk to me anyday. I feel so shame. My mother, I never want to hurt her. She so many times had trouble with my father like I have trouble with Raul now. My father was a soldier. She thinks I am like my father and she don't talk to me. Like with father, she pushes away the whole family. She makes like mute. I

187

am learn that from story about a girl who can't talk. Also mute is the name for making the violin quiet. Rain's sister told me this. She plays all day, violin, violin. Always I think of Rain house, I hear violin. Maybe I go there now when we are out of suspension. Rain and me talk a lot in suspension time. He is good, just weak. I am weak too but nobody see. His sister is very stronger.

--

February 8

Rain

All the applications are in. I will get out of this fucking town if it's the last thing I do. I wish there were another means of escape besides college Ms. Drummond but if there is, I can't think of it. That's what boys like me do, right?

I went to get HIV tested the other day, by the way. Drove to Oceanside in my dad's car (which broke down on the way back cause apparently the man who sold it to him neglected to mention that it had been completely submerged in water. Yes that's right, the car my dad bought had been UNDERWATER). Luckily this is why he has AAA. But when I wasn't back in time I had to think of why I was on my way back from Oceanside and I said I was seeing an experimental theater production. WHAT EXPERIMENTAL THEATRE IS IN OCEANSIDE? My parents didn't even bat an eye.

So I'm there at that dirty clinic getting blood drawn, and the nurse is singing "He's only seventeen" to me, but adding lyrics about STDS. She gave me an envelope of pamphlets and some lube and a fist full of condoms and sent me on my way. Now the wait begins. I would kill myself if I did anything to hurt Faruq.

--

February 14

Rain

188

Ms. Drummond, you bitch!

--

February 20

Rain

Sorry. I didn't mean that. Ok, maybe a little.

--

March 1

Rain

Yeah, that was harsh. I'd cross it out, but now it's clear you've been reading all along, so I have nothing to hide. (Watch out.) Ok, so now we've established that I'm not actually suicidal. Also, as my previous entry demonstrated, I take care of myself. I mean, I'm not out here giving everybody AIDS, I actually got checked and of course I'm fine. Maybe you should have talked to me before you reported it to Mr. Hendlin? Did you maybe have a moment of hysterical homophobia, Ms. Drummond? Just think about that. My shrink told me that when he was a kid you could kill someone and then get off by saying that you had "temporary insanity due to homosexual confusion." (I made a note of it just in case I'd need it later.) Seriously? You thought I would be a danger to myself? How many of these do you read? I can only imagine you've read that before. Why only freak out when the fag waxes suicidal? Just think about it.

But, while we're oversharing (remember you asked for it) it was kinda illuminating. After the whole "danger assessment" bullshit was over, they got me to the counselor, Ms. Shapiro. Do you know about her? Do you know she was in a sex cult? Hahahaah. Well, you're gonna now! (I warned you!) So, the first day I started at this wretched high school, I walked right up to Ms. Shapiro and said, "Oh hi Shinyam! I didn't know you worked here!" She kinda shushed me and said, "They call me Ms. Shapiro here." All those years of key parties and

189

hashish orgies with my parents and the whole time I had no idea she was a high school guidance counselor! You know my parents are hippies and all but she went ALL THE WAY with that cult shit. She even tried to get them into it. Do you know what the people in that cult did? Our own Ms. Shapiro used to be part of a "community" whose primary spiritual practice was to put people in a room, turn off all the lights and like, let them all fuck like animals. Put that in your pipe and smoke it in the teachers' lounge, Ms. Drummond.

--

April 10
                    Faruq
I lose credit for not writing the Diary for so long time. I don't feel to write it. Ramadan month. And my brain hurt. My brain it hurts. Too much English. I learn so much the first year, second year. Now I'm tired. I like to play a new video game I got. But I read. I am reading. I like the books you gave. My English getting better with reading. I know you read all now, Ms. Drummond. Rain told me this. This also why I don't write. I shy to write. You know he's not crazy. Just wild. I am wild too. I never knew before. Not so easy that others see my wild in Iraq. There everybody is wild in their mind but everybody have a place in home and life. Here nobody have no place in home, no place in life, so wild in mind is easy to see. Now everybody who had problems with another in Iraq before the war have easy time to kill the other. Saddam keep everyone down. Saddam KEPT everyone down. Now everyone is wild without Saddam.

--

May 4
                    Rain
We went to the beach today. I mean, we went to THAT beach, if you know what I mean. We were a hit. (Listen, if

190

you can't handle reading these then don't.). We had to fight the old trolls off, it was like a convention of gawkers. Faruq wouldn't swim naked. I did. And I know he thinks he hated it, but he loved watching me skinny dip. Oh my god, I AM my mother, provacatrice extraordinaire. We even held hands for a while, like we do at night, walking along the shore. A guy said he was writer and he wanted to know our story. Faruq told him— I'll never forget this for the rest of my writing life—Faruq told him, "I write my own story."

--

May 10

Rain

Le printempts et ici et tout mon sang et dans ma bit. Ms. Ramey-Foucade is teaching us some choice French! Thank god for that old fag-hag's class. And yours.

Are you writing a novel, Ms. Drummond? Would you use this as material? I swear I'll sue.

No really, thank you. You're the only teacher I can remember who ever stopped kids from saying "fag" in class. Mr. Althausen even said it himself. "No fags in my class" he said, and I wondered if I could disappear into my jacket like A Wrinkle in Time.

We were at the beach again the other night. Me and Leah and Faruq. We went to a bonfire with some punks from Vista. It was a great time, probably because of the tequila. The cops came, but we already had a hole dug for the booze so all they could do was break up the party. So afterwards we're drunk and looking for trouble and the three of us are sitting there, backs to the boardwalk, gazing out at the waves and suddenly we notice that there's like a bunch of people surrounding us. We would have been much more scared if we weren't so drunk. I'm like, what the hell? Then I notice they have their arms out, like they're casting a spell or something. You know what they were doing? Praying! Praying for us, or on us, or something. Like who just walks around in a pack, looking for kids to pray over?

So I'm drunk and feeling punk and I'm like, "I do not approve of this. You do not have my permission to pray for me." But they just keep it up. Now the old one (he's like thirty or something, the rest are kids) is praying out loud, bible verses about lying with a man as with a women, and Faruq's like "let's get out of here" and I totally should have. Leah thought it was hilarious and frankly, she was egging me on. But Faruq. I'd never seen him like that. He was, I don't know, like he disappeared. Not like he physically ran away—that was later. He was just there/not there. Know what I mean? There was so much going on...

I get up and I'm like shouting at them now, screaming "Stop praying! Stop your fucking praying!" And they're louder and louder and then they kind of link hands, so we're trapped. So Leah and I link our hands and surround Faruq and start intoning some spell we heard in the movie Excalibur, "Anel natrach uthbath bethus dochyel dyenye" and doing this whole Exorcist thing with the whites of our eyes. Then Faruq is gone. He'd fought his way out and dived into the waves. Now I'm trying to get past their arms and almost did, but then I realize Leah's still there. Now she's freaking out and I sort of blanked out until it was over. All I remember is the Christers walking away down the boardwalk and one of them screaming "God hates fags!" We went looking for Faruq up and down the beach but he was nowhere.

--

May 14

Faruq

So strange here. Stranger now. Leah is smart with me. She say she knows everythings. She tells me I need to

192

help Rain. Says Rain was sad because I act like friend with him. I am a friend! My only friend here is Rain and Leah. Carlos my manager, you are my teacher. How I should be different? She can't tell me. Says I don't know what I do. What I should do? Mother is not angry with me like before but she acts different. Say I need to work more shifts, not staying everytime with Leah and Rain. She thinks Leah is a bad woman. I have no other friend! Other students don't talk to me, don't talk to Rain either. Leah talks to everyone.

--

May 17

Rain

I was not my best self this weekend, Ms. Drummond. Not my best self at all. I probably shouldn't have stolen the beer in the first place, but it seemed like the thing to do at the time. Stealing from poor Mexicans aside, it was not a healthy choice. Faruq and I were in the flowers again, doing our thing, whatever it means to him. Anyway, right there, clean and pristine between the dirty carpet strips and tamale husks was this cold, 24-pack of coronas. As I said, it seemed like the thing to do at the time. We took it up the hill to Leah's and just started drinking. Her mom's never home and she's got that chiminea thing in the backyard. (It was super cinematographic!) None of us had eaten and Faruq never drinks. Somehow we finished most of them. And somehow we all ended up naked. We took some photos—very artistic!—and then, well, then Faruq and Leah got kinda frisky. I could have said something. I can always say something. I know that. But I never do. Instead, I left. I don't know what happened. I don't want to.

--

May 18

Faruq

193

Fatma is talking to a boy. I know this. Mother doesn't know. I listen in the telephone line when they're talking. I will stop them all the talking now. I have only little things to do here, work for the money, help mother, be the father of the house. I must to take care of this. They are talking love.

--

May 25

Faruq

Everyone is talking about College now. Everyone is ready for leave Encinitas. I don't know. I can go to community college easy, so I will wait. Easy to enter later. Now so many things happening and family is most important. I know Ms. Shapiro want college now for me, but I don't want to take a far away college. This is impossible for me. But sometime I think to try and go far.

--

June 3

Faruq

Graduation is coming. I made the picture and payed for clothes but maybe I don't go. I feel to hide. Mother doesn't worry about my graduation. She doesn't know I have many classes to complete still. Leah helps me with classes. I can't do all the work without her, only math. We don't have financial papers for the FASAF and is easier to pay the community college simply than all the documents. Fatma is a perfect student. So good, so better than me. I am very proud like father and brother for her.

--

June 10

Rain

Leah and I met that guy at the beach again, the lead Christer, the older one. He came up and was trying to chat us up about the good news. Leah took off. It was too much for her. I was gonna follow, but I had to ask about

194

his face! Dude. There was a huge wound across it, a long gash from his cheek up to his forehead. "What happened?" I asked. He said it was an accident at work. "Something flew off the machine," he said. I almost smiled but I caught myself.

Faruq's being weird. He kinda disappears more and more. Like he's there one second, then he's like out of it. And he's always looking over his shoulder. Leah and him have been hanging out. It bothered me for a while but after that night at in the park, well, I guess it's simpler. I didn't write about that yet. Damn. Leaving things out. Not the way to write a diary!

Well, he ended up in the emergency room. Faruq, that is. Don't worry, he wasn't hurt. And somehow he charmed the old Persian doctor, who somehow spoke Arabic, into not calling his mom. It's weird, he had kind of a bad trip on pot. Like, when we were in the park, everything was cool for a while—lots of laughing until we cried, cheeks hurting kind of stupid stuff—then all of a sudden (it was his first time trying weed) he just freaked out. First he saw all these shapes in the bushes (we were down deep in Torrey Pines, in the ravine where everyone drops acid) and then he was sure his mother knew what he was doing, kept talking about how ashamed he was. He's gotten weird like before, but usually after sex, and frankly, we haven't done anything like that in a while. That kind of thing just...evaporated one day for him. I mean, I got the signal. And I just stopped pushing it. Anyway, I thought he had calmed down when I left him near his place—he always wants to be dropped off a block away. I guess he turned around and walked himself all the way to the ER. He thought there was something wrong with the weed. Thought it was giving him a heart attack. That was pretty much the last time we hung out.

Maybe it's better. To be totally honest, I feel more in my

skin now. Now that everything's back to the shitty old normal. Last week I met a guy on the beach. He lives in Temecula but he's got a car. He picked me up on Friday and we drove into the city. He knows the clubs where they don't check IDs.

I'm still waiting to find out about my conditional acceptance. Man if I could do it all over again, I'd have listened to the counselors about the FAFSA. But I think they didn't realize how fucked up my family is. I guess we look a certain way from the outside. Dad and I had to drink a bottle of whisky just to get the docs together. It is phenomenally sad to see how deeply he has fucked himself financially. Of course he didn't want to face it.

--

June 15

Faruq

Graduation today. I'm not there in the morning. I have a meeting with the man who gives us a chance for business. Very good man, he is like us how we got here. He has restaurant is very good, very success in El Cajon. My father is the same tribe so he will help us here. He let me use his car and we make trips to pick up goods from stores in Oceanside, bring to Cajon. There are many more Iraquis in El Cajon. Some have houses they rent. Some buy houses and rent others. Maybe my whole family will move to El Cajon.

--

June 21

Rain

Berkeley is a go! Wait list OVER! As long as I complete Algebra II in community college this summer, I'm in. Got some good financial aid too. Apparently, we're poorer than we act. As it turns out, it's supremely doable! So, I'm getting out. Out. I can breathe again.

--

196

June 7

Faruq

It is simple in Iraq. Very wild, but more simpler. Everything has a place. And something has no place, so is easier. Man doesn't touch woman, so man touch man, no problem. Just don't talk. Here, talk is everything. Everythings have a name and name is bad. I tell this to Rain. He says he understands, no problem, but I don't think so he understands. I know why not. Leah is staying here next year. My family is happy again. Fatma is marry soon.

Darren Chase teaches English at New Design High, a public school in his Lower East Side neighborhood. An accomplished opera singer, he has released several recordings of classical art songs, winning The American Prize for his album, *The Young Debussy*. He is the author of *Singing from the Inside*, a manual of vocal technique and *Mindfulness for Teens,* a course in meditation and mindfulness for high school students. His translation of Wilhelm Müller's *Die Winterreise* is used for English-language performances of Schubert's song cycle all over the world. He studies writing with Bruce Benderson.

(http://darrenchase.net/)

Choice

[after hearing a recording of "I am Metis" by Deb Voss]

By

Natalie Reid

Those who write "I did not choose" cry pain in their throat,
weep grief.
Those who whisper "I did not choose" bear witness to atrocity,
reveal deep scars.
Those who shout "I did not choose" reclaim their ancestry,
circle back to beginnings.

But I, who once spoke that tongue,
have lost the words,
which fled in the night, tiptoeing,
leaving me breathless.

Seeking air,
I began to choose, finding
in each small choice
the language of the chooser,
the voice of the chosen.

I now choose to speak the words

    I know

    I can

    I will

I choose to disagree

when what I hear needs refuting

and to answer back

when what I hear causes harm.

I choose to wear color

in the land of black garments,

wear turquoise

in the city of diamonds,

wear clothes that don't match because

I like them that way.

I choose to say "I am a mystic"

in a roomful of scholars

and "I am a skeptic"

to those who cling to belief

so as not to risk thinking.

I choose to carry all of myself

wherever I go,

at all hours of the sun

and in all visions of the moon,

I choose

I choose

I choose

—and that which I did not choose,

whatever it was,

has flown on the wind and is gone.

Natalie Reid has always preferred Oz to Aunt Em's home and has always made her living on the road, first teaching English in Japan and the Pacific, and now in northern Europe and Russia. Natalie also teaches writing in the mythological voice and other writing workshops at the confluence of creativity and spirituality.

The Past Keeps Changing (For Chana Bloch)

By

Alison Jennings

After you died, you spoke out loud,

Chana,

from the obituary pages.

I'm glad I found you, while avidly reading thumbnail

sketches of the recently departed.

Don't laugh—it's necessary research, since my body's

aging without permission.

Like an aberrant tumor, I have a burgeoning interest

in how we're measured posthumously.

You would understand such obsession, would tell me

not to come in out of the rain.

Like Solomon—sagely determining whose child it is—

you assigned simplicity to life's

surprises, not shying from searing mysteries of love,

or the humbling downfall of the body.

You zapped me like a taser when you admitted:

We learn through intuitions and confusions, but we deny

and delay, and finally discover who we are.

Now the moon is almost full, Chana,

floating towards the heavens.

(Note: The Moon Is Almost Full is Chana Bloch's last book.)

Alison Jennings is a Seattle-based poet who taught in public schools before returning to poetry. She has also worked as editor, journalist, and accountant. Close to 60 of her poems have been published internationally in numerous journals, including *Burningword, Cathexis Northwest Press, Meat for Tea, Mslexia, Poetic Sun, The Raw Art Review,* and *The Write Launch.* She has won 3rd Place/Honorable Mention or been a semi-finalist in several contests.

Please visit her website at

https://sites.google.com/view/airandfirepoet/home.

Acknowledgements

Many thanks to Charles Templeton of the Writers' Colony at Dairy Hollow in Eureka Springs, Arkansas for his assistance in procuring submissions for this book. Without his help, my efforts at compiling this anthology would have been difficult. I would also like to thank the authors who so unselfishly provided their intellectual property in order to make a contribution to St. Jude Children's Research Hospital. Many of the authors are affiliated with The Writer's Colony; others are located in other parts of the country and overseas, making this an international effort. I am grateful for your kindness and compassion.

S.F.L.

Printed in Great Britain
by Amazon